CRITICAL ACCLAIM FOR THE DUFFY MYSTERIES

"In *The Comeback*, Tom Schreck's good-guy Duffy Dombrowski continues his journey of helping those who can't help themselves. He even helps them after they're dead. Readers who are addicted to Lee Child's Jack Reacher protag will appreciate Duffy, who is tougher than the violent bad guys he faces down. A fun, muscular read."

—G. Miki Hayden, author of *Writing the Mystery*

"Duffy Dombrowski, the hero of Tom Schreck's *The Comeback*, is the kind of guy you can count on if your car breaks down at 3am, you need a last-minute sparring partner at the gym, or you're a few dollars short for your next whiskey. I'm glad I got to hang out with him."

—Tim O'Mara, author of the Raymond Donne series

"*The Vegas Knockout* is a funny book, full of engaging characters that cover the spectrum of human likeability. What makes it more than a piece of fluff is how Schreck uses Duffy's love of boxing to stand in for any devotion truly held. Duffy's success is in his journey, just as the greatest fun in *The Vegas Knockout* is in the reading."

—Dana King, author of the Penns River Crime Novels

"*Out Cold* floored me with a quick one two of the serious and seriously funny. Schreck's unique blending of the absurd and the sublime along with his rather oddball cast of characters makes *Out Cold* a great read."

—Reed Farrel Coleman, two-time Shamus Award winning author of *Empty Ever After*

"Fresh, intense and funny, Schreck's second mystery to feature unrepentant Elvis fan and dog lover Duffy Dombrowski packs a knockout punch."

—*Publishers Weekly*, for *TKO*

"Refreshingly iconoclastic."

—*Kirkus Reviews*, for *TKO*

"*TKO* is fast-paced, authentic, and funny as hell. Social worker and journeyman boxer Duffy Dombrowski is a workingman's hero, and I want him in my corner!"

—Sean Chercover, author of *Trinity Game*

"Not since Carl Hiassen's *Tourist Season* debut has there been a novel with such superb comic timing and laugh-out-loud lines."

—Ken Bruen, Shamus Award-winning author of *The Guards*, for *On the Ropes*

"An Everyman with a big heart and a wicked jab, Duffy Dombrowski may well be the new Spenser. I can't wait for Round Two."

—Marcus Sakey, author of *The Blade Itself*, for *On the Ropes*

"*On the Ropes* is sly, funny, irreverent, and one hell of a good time. Read it or be sorry you didn't. It's just that simple."

—Laurien Berenson, author of *Hounded to Death*

"It'll put you down for the count with laughter. Tom Schreck is a contender for funniest author working in the crime genre today."

—William Kent Krueger, author of *Thunder Bay*, for *On the Ropes*

THE COMEBACK

BOOKS BY TOM SCHRECK

The Duffy Dombrowski Mysteries
On the Ropes
TKO
Out Cold
The Vegas Knockout
The Ten Count
The Comeback

Getting Dunn
Redeeming Trace

Join "Duffy's Fight Club" for free short thrillers, an audio book, Tom's magazine work, a video on judging boxing, Tom's appearance on "Copy Cat Killers" and Rocky the blood hound singing "My Way." TomSchreck.com.

TOM SCHRECK

THE COMEBACK

A Duffy Mystery

Down & Out Books
3959 Van Dyke Road, Suite 265
Lutz, FL 33558
DownAndOutBooks.com

Cover design by Pixelstudio

ISBN: 1-64396-326-0
ISBN-13: 978-1-64396-326-6

Chapter One

"AJ is dead," Jerry said. I just got to the phone before it went to voicemail.

"What?" I was half awake, hadn't had any coffee yet, and Al, my basset hound, started barking. That set off Agnes, the bloodhound I'm minding, into a baying.

"What the hell are you talking about? What happened?"

"He was closing up last night after we all left, and he must've had a heart attack behind the bar. Dmitri found him when he came in to clean," Jerry said. AJ owned and ran AJ's, a bar that Jerry, who goes by Jerry Number Two, and I, and a few other men frequent on a nightly basis.

"What do we do? Did he have any family?" The question felt sad and out of place and I was a little embarrassed, asking it. I saw AJ almost every night of my adult life and he was almost always miserable. I often said it looked like he had a stomachache that had lasted the seventeen years he'd owned the place. He didn't like Al in the bar, though he never really refused him, and he stocked the cooler with Schlitz because I drank it, but I knew very little about the man.

"He was originally from Chicago and he had a grown daughter in her thirties. He mentioned her once or twice, but they had some sort of falling out. He hadn't heard from her in years," Jerry said.

Al transitioned from barking into the piercing whining that

always went through my head like an ice pick. Agnes didn't like it either and pawed him between the eyes. Al did the turbo basset thing and flung slobber all around and Agnes mooed at him. I put the phone on speaker and filled their dishes while I kept the conversation going with Jerry.

"The other guys know?" I asked. The other guys were TC, Rocco and the other Jerry, known as Jerry Number One.

"Yeah. Dmitri had Rocco's number and he was the first to know. He called T-C and Jerry, and Jerry called me," he said.

I didn't know what else to say. The five of us didn't see each other outside the bar very often, if ever. We drank together and held drinking conversations. We liked each other and we were friends, but in that way men are friends. We didn't go to each-others' houses on Thanksgiving or to kids' first communions or anything like that.

"Duff? You still there?" Jerry said.

"Yeah, yeah, Jerry. I'm here. I guess I was just thinking," I said.

"I know what you mean." Jerry paused. "Hey, Duff?"

"Yeah, Jer," I said.

"What do we do now?" Jerry said.

"I don't know," I said.

The dogs finished their meals. Al stood at his bowl. His ears were wet from drinking out of the toilet and he varied his glance from his bowl to me. He wanted more. Al always wanted more. Agnes went back to her bed, spun around three times and collapsed like a building being imploded. I grabbed their leashes, which set Al off in a different way and he ran at me, jumping up and bouncing his meaty front paws off my thighs. I got him hooked up on the first try and Agnes strolled over. She was more polite, and I easily got her to sit, and then we left the Airstream.

We headed down Route 9 and I let Al dictate the pace. A friend of mine once said walking Al was like walking a vacuum cleaner. His pace matched the interest his nose had in his surroundings. If Al was driven by some invisible scent he might linger or he might dart after whatever stinking thing caught his fancy. Otherwise, he just sniffed and barely waddled.

At one hundred and forty pounds, Agnes could be a challenge if she caught a scent she wanted to pursue. Other times, especially if her belly was full, she could just match Al's pace and sniff her way along.

Today was a sniff and waddle day.

It gave me time to think, which is almost never a good thing for me. A guy I saw every night for seventeen years was dead and I didn't know how to feel. I was shocked, I felt sad but other than that, I couldn't identify emotions. I tried to think of great times or AJ nostalgia and I hated the feeling that I was forcing it. It felt like something was wrong with me that that was all I felt. Either that or there was something wrong with life.

The thing was, my friend was dead. How I felt wasn't going to change that and I knew I was powerless to do anything. I also had to walk the hounds, pick up their shit and then go to work. There was no punctuation mark that I could put around AJ's death. Life kept on going at the same speed.

That is something I didn't understand and probably never would.

Chapter Two

Not only had a friend died but it was also a Tuesday, the morning I had to meet with the clinic's director, Claudia Michelin. She was a bureaucrat who loved the minutiae of regulations and thrived on her ability to lord over me and the other staff with her dictums. I've worked as a counselor for more than a decade and have had my share of verbal, written, and last-chance warnings, but I've always found a way to escape. Sometimes I was able to pull something off and sometimes the stars just lined up and I got a break.

Claudia told me on Friday that she was doing a chart audit of my case files and that we'd go over them during supervision. I might come out okay if I got lucky and she pulled out the right files that I had up to date, but when I thought about how many I really had that were up to date, I became less confident about my chances. Just the same, I'd find a way to survive, I always did.

Trina, the office manager, was back from maternity leave. She and I had some complicated history but now that she was married and had a baby girl and I had whatever I had with a girl called TJ, we had settled into a somewhat comfortable platonic friendship that simply ignored our past. I didn't understand it, but I respected her and her marriage and never wanted to threaten that or suggest anything that would make Trina feel weird about anything. Joseph, not Joe, her husband, knew only that we were workmates.

"Duff, she picked bad ones," Trina said, referring to the charts Claudia had reviewed. Trina made a pained face.

"How bad?' I asked.

"Real bad ones. Robinson's, Kareem's and Latanya's," Trina said.

Those were not only bad, they were my absolute worst. I had done weekly sessions with them and I had followed up with reports that got them their social services benefits, but I hadn't written treatment plans or session notes that were due a month ago; no, more like two months ago.

That made me bad at what I did but no matter how I tried to give a shit, I didn't care enough to actually do the charting work. I didn't care enough about paperwork.

I did care about the people and I think they knew it. Unfortunately, the job had always been about paperwork and since the insurance companies had started dictating things, it had gotten much worse. Even when I tried to care, I just couldn't.

So, it was going to be a shit show where Claudia got to feel good about herself by telling me how irresponsible I was and how disappointed in me she was. I'd be okay. I'd get another double secret probation and I'd promise to never let it happen again. I might have to do a couple of all-nighters to get the charts caught up, but as much as that sucked, I had done it many times before.

I checked my email just to have something to do before my ass-kicking. I felt my stomach twist and my throat tighten when I saw an email from tdunn@us.homelandsecurity.gov. It was TJ, and I hadn't heard from her in a few weeks. She usually worked at a strip joint in Crawford called The Taco, but the Army had called her back into active duty for an indeterminate length of time. The callup had come during a period when we were trying to figure out where our relationship was headed. TJ carried around a lot of emotional baggage that wasn't her fault, but it frequently left me guessing where I stood with her, often with a broken heart to boot.

The email read:

Duff, I'm going to stay on this assignment. They said I could leave but, though it is hard to explain, I think I'm better off here than back in Crawford. That's not fair to you, I know, but it is what I have to do. Please try to understand and live your life as if I wasn't part of it. T

I felt the air sucked out of me. I got a little lightheaded and it was tough to swallow. I had a moment where I couldn't tell whether what was happening was real. I didn't cry, though I wish, in a way, that I had. It just felt surreal and too terribly real, all at the same time.

"You know, Duffy, it's bad enough that your performance has been so problematic lately, but you compound things by being late for a scheduled supervisory meeting," I heard Claudia say. She was in the doorway of my cubicle, scowling at me with her hands on her hips.

I looked away from my computer and into her eyes.

"What did you say?" I asked.

She did a contrived sigh of disapproval and started to talk.

I didn't let her. In one motion I stood up and hurled my desk into the wall in front of me. It made a chaotic violent sound and Claudia jumped back. I picked up the desktop monitor and threw it and I heard glass shatter and saw sparks fly as it showered the office.

"Take this job, those charts and your fucking condescending attitude and stick them up your ass!" I said. I glared at her, my eyes on fire and my chest heaving. Claudia had stepped back and had a look of terror in her eyes. "You hear me! You don't have power over me, and you never have! Fuck you, fuck you, fuck you!"

I grabbed my coat and my car keys and walked past her, grabbing the files out of her hand and throwing them down the hallway as I headed for the door. I passed Trina's desk on my way out.

"Oh my God, Duffy..." I heard her say out loud, but not really to me.

Chapter Three

I could hear my heartbeat and I felt my palms sweat. Even though I had fantasized about doing exactly what I had just done thousands of times, there's a world of difference between the safety of pretending and the reality of action. Action had consequences and real uncertainty.

There were folks who told people off all the time. In lots of ways, I admired them but then when I thought about their station in life, they were usually guys who worked in gyms or hung out in bars or had just got out of the county jail. I've always thought how freeing it would be to have their attitude.

Now, I had no source of income and the bridge I had just crossed was on fire. Honestly, I was a little scared but somewhere inside I also felt a little okay, like ten years was too long to put up with something and money wasn't reason enough to keep swallowing shit. The emphasis there is on "a little okay" and also somewhere deep down inside.

Right now, there was also the challenge of finding something to do. I don't do well with idle time; my mind races, my thoughts get weird and I have problems sorting things out. I'm much better in motion but with a whole day in front of me I wasn't sure what kind of motion to be in. It was too early to drink, and AJ's wasn't open yet, or, more accurately, was out of business.

I went to the Crawford Y and decided to go to the boxing room, even though it would be deserted. It was the closest thing

I had to a home away from home. In the afternoon and early evening, it would fill up with the characters that make up boxing gyms: fighters, wannabe fighters, coaches, cut men and guys who just liked being around boxing gyms. It was kind of like the way men liked barbershops. It was a masculine place where guys could be men and be tough.

The funny thing is, guys who actually fought, the guys who actually got in the ring, didn't need a lot of masculine affirmation. Fighters are pretty comfortable in their manhood. I think much of the bullshit posturing that men do is a substitute for real fighting. They constantly try to measure themselves against other men by looking at money, women, cars, jobs, you-name-it. Guys who have fought for years leave that shit behind.

Real fighters also don't care if women want to share the gym as fighters or just to get a workout. The fighters don't bitch about how women don't belong there. Now, the wanna-bees, on the other hand, usually are the ones making noise about how the gym is no place for women and wannabes are the obnoxious assholes you run into in the street who do all the woofing and hollering about how tough they are. In the gym, fighters look at them and shake their heads.

None of this, by the way, is ever spoken. I've been fighting as an amateur and a pro for almost thirty years. In my pro career, I lose just as much as I win. I beat most of the guys I should beat, local guys and most average regional guys. I get my ass kicked when I win a few in a row and I get matched up with an up-and-coming stud.

I know my place.

A couple of years back I took a few too many headshots and my trainer wouldn't let me fight any more until I got a battery of tests. I did, and they came back pretty normal, though the neurologist said that dementia stuff often took years, even decades, to show up.

I flicked on the lights and waited while the old-school fluorescents hummed and crackled and came on. I took a deep breath and let the gym's years of sweat and funk waft through my nostrils like a good soup's seasoning. I got my jump rope out of my locker; it was the kind made up of string and hard plastic sections. I switched to this type a few months ago and I liked it because it gave the rope some weight. I put on the old boom box and got out the cassette tape of Elvis cuts. "The Promised Land," "Burning Love" and "I Washed My Hands in Muddy Water" were my favorites to skip to.

Elvis had just got "*Outta Luuuusiana and on to Houston Town...*" when Smitty, the guy who had run the Y's boxing program for thirty-five years, came down the stairs.

"Why the hell ain't you at work?" Smitty said by way of greeting.

That was Smitty.

He was seventy-something, Black, and Dartmouth-educated, though you wouldn't guess that. I didn't know it until I'd been here twenty years.

"Uh, I just, uh, resigned," I said. I knew he wouldn't be pleased.

"Tell me it is because you got a better opportunity and not that you went and told that woman off," Smitty said. He knew me better than I knew me.

I didn't say anything. I knew better than to bullshit Smitty.

Smitty shook his head in disgust. "You got a plan?" he asked.

"It just happened this morning." I hesitated. "I'll be fine."

Smitty just looked at me.

I waited for a moment and then tried to change the subject.

"What are you doing here so early?" I asked.

He took a deep breath and slowly let it out.

"My brother died. He has an autistic son down in South Carolina. I gotta go take care of him," Smitty said.

I felt something in my stomach. It was something I hadn't felt when I walked out of my job. I hadn't felt it when I'd heard the news about AJ, either. But somehow I could tell—I don't know how I could tell—that Smitty wasn't coming back.

"When you leavin'?" I asked.

"After I grab my things," he said, and nodded toward his small office.

I'd had to ask, even though I already knew the answer.

"When you comin' back?"

He shook his head. He looked down at the tile floor. He looked up at his office.

"I talked to Al." Al was the YMCA's executive director. "I told him I wanted you to be in charge."

"What? Like until you come back? I can do that. What do you figure, a few weeks?"

Smitty shook his head and walked over to his office.

"Keep everything in here. My old gloves—I wore them for twenty years when I trained—and the old-school headgear... Do me a favor. Don't throw them out." Smitty just looked at them on the shelf, which also held a half-dozen trophies from his amateur career and the photo of him fighting in a Madison Square Garden main event. The fight had been declared a draw and he never got the shot at the title, but he considered this his biggest moment.

I felt sick to my stomach. I was going to cry, and I didn't want to do it in front of him. He was a father to me.

"I'm not running the gym," I said. I looked down. It just didn't feel right.

Smitty nodded and didn't say anything.

He put some papers in a bag and headed to the exit. He stopped to say something.

"You know, Duff, you don't know what life is going to throw at you. What you can do is control how you respond. Shakespeare said something about it. Sometimes you're born with shit and sometimes it is what you decide to make out of it." He turned toward me and looked me in the eye. "Take care of yourself, Duff. You're a good man."

He turned back around and walked out.

Chapter Four

I didn't stay at the gym, I couldn't.

I didn't have any desire to be in charge of the gym. That wasn't my place—that was Smitty's place. It didn't make any sense to me to take that on.

I went home to take Agnes and Al for another walk and poured myself a bourbon into my "Short Legs, Big Heart" basset coffee mug. I don't know what other people use alcohol for, but I use it to quiet my self-talk. Maybe it was from years of counseling or maybe it was just in my genes or maybe it was all a grand rationalization for not wanting to feel uncomfortable emotions, but I couldn't stop things from going around in my head. My thoughts ran around and around, and I often couldn't make sense of them. I think this current internal dialogue made my point perfectly.

My iPhone played Elvis's "Long Black Limousine" into my headphones as I balanced the two leashes and my refreshment. I had given up on trying to look good during this activity and bought myself an army surplus belt and a big carabiner hook to fasten to the leashes. A couple of spilled bourbons had been the mother of this invention. Strutting down the route I lived on with two hounds strapped to my belt, sipping a coffee mug full of bourbon, was quite a look and I didn't have to wonder why women didn't stop and hurl themselves at me.

Elvis was singing about all his dreams, traveling in the back of that limousine. It is at the end of the last verse of the song that we find out the limo was really a hearse, and he was mourning the loss of a girlfriend who had died in the big city, chasing her dreams. It wasn't a subtle selection, but my mind was too busy to seek out the vagaries of something else. It wasn't four o'clock yet and I'd lost a friend, a girlfriend, a hangout, a job and the closest thing I ever had to a mentor. The day stung and it left me confused and existentially fucked up. The Jim Beam without ice or water stung only a little as it went down my gullet.

"*I'm sorry now, Girl, but I must leave you...*" Elvis sang as "You'll Think of Me" followed "Long Black Limousine" on the 1968 playlist I'd put together. Elvis could put more emotion into a song than even the best lyrics deserved, or at least he did for me. Since I was little, Elvis had expressed my emotions for me or at least helped me to feel mine. It was difficult to explain, so most of the time I didn't, but it was the thing in my life that I was certain about and I didn't have to check with anyone else. Probably the only thing I was certain about.

The music went quiet for an instant and I knew a call was interrupting my Elvis/Jim Beam reverie.

"Hey Duff, It's Jerry," my friend said. It was Jerry Number Two.

"What's up, Man?" I said.

"AJ's daughter is in town and wants to meet the five of us at the bar tonight at seven," Jerry said.

"Really?" I didn't quite get it. "You have an idea why?"

"No, none of us does but I'm not sure if AJ had other people in his life. Maybe she just wants to meet us," Jerry said.

I took a second to sip and to think.

"Okay, then I guess I'll see you at the bar," I said. We hung up, I took another pull of Beam, noted that the sting was gone, and headed home to feed the hounds. Life was just getting weirder by the hour. I showered and got ready to head to the bar.

***

I felt like I was going to a wake. The more I thought about it, I wondered if I was. I parked the El Dorado right out front and noticed the other guys' cars. I checked my watch and it was just seven but then realized the Fearsome Foursome, as they had come to be known, were probably consumed with worry over what was going to happen to their clubhouse and just had to get there early.

The place felt different from the second I walked in. For one thing, the lights were up, and the brightness gave the usually dark, shadowed place an antiseptic feel, almost like it was a museum piece or TV set. The other odd thing was that the four guys were quiet. That was *really* odd.

A thirtyish woman, not unattractive but not pretty, either, was behind the bar with a guy in a wrinkled suit. She had a short, bobbed hairdo, a cream complexion and a kind of bitter mouth. The guy looked familiar but who he was didn't immediately come to me. I took my usual spot at the bar, one seat removed from TC.

"Hi, I'm Amy Ackhurst, Arnold's daughter," the woman behind the bar said. She must've read my expression. "AJ, I'm sorry." Her lips were tight and her forehead a bit wrinkled. She wore a plain green crew-neck sweater over a white turtleneck and newish Levi's. She seemed annoyed.

She looked at the guy in the wrinkled suit. He was bald and had that weird combination of being skinny around most of his body and fat at the gut. The nose had been broken and his wire-framed glasses were crooked.

"Let's start," she said. Her voice didn't carry any particular emotion.

"Hi, everyone. My name is Phillip Fowler, and I am the attorney for Miss Ackhurst, Arnold's sole heir."

Phillip Fowler?

This was the clown that the court assigned to me when I got

jammed up in Las Vegas. He was like the absent-minded professor's more absent-minded, less stylish, brother.

"Fowler?" I said, interrupting things.

That seemed to startle him.

"Mister Dombrowski," he gave me a noncommittal nod.

He made no eye contact with anyone. He didn't seem nervous or concerned with his delivery or appearance. "I am here because Arnold requested that Amy and I be present at this meeting. He wanted us here as soon as possible after he passed, and it was with considerable effort that we got her here so quickly," he said. Amy looked at her watch and sighed some annoyance without doing much to conceal it.

"He knew how important this place of business was to you five. He wanted it to have a chance to continue without him," He looked at Amy for the first time. She nodded. "Amy was given the choice of taking over the establishment—"

Amy interrupted. "I have no desire to do that. My life isn't here and I, frankly, have no interest in the bar business, or for that matter, my father's old life. He left my mother when I was very young, and we've never had any contact with him since. I split my time between Chicago and Galway Lake, just north of here." She wasn't looking at us or even the attorney. Her speech seemed rehearsed and it didn't carry much emotion with it, except for annoyance.

"Considering that," Fowler continued, "Arnold had put a provision in his estate for the establishment to continue." He paused and for a moment and looked at us. "He has left the bar, the business, the second- and third-floor apartments and the rest of the building to Duffy Dombrowski, with the provision that Mister Dombrowski agree to continue to operate it."

I felt all the eyes in the room on me. I wasn't sure what I had heard; it didn't seem real.

"Excuse me?" I heard come out of my mouth.

"The place is yours if you want it," Amy said. "I don't mean to be rude, but I need to know now. I want to get back home, and

I want all this shit behind me," Amy said. She was caring even less now about hiding her annoyance.

What did I know about the bar business? I knew it from one side of the bar. Why would I want this? This wasn't for me. Oh God, no.

I looked at the Foursome. They said nothing and just looked at me. I couldn't think. I couldn't process things. They needed the place.

Shit, maybe I needed the place. I needed a place to drink, not a place to own and run.

They just continued to look at me.

I did what I did when I felt like this. I acted on instinct.

"Yeah, I'll take it," I said.

As that came out of my mouth I thought of my not-so-great track history with acting on my instincts.

Chapter Five

I signed a few forms, a couple of official-looking documents, and when that was done she handed me a check for five thousand dollars. .

"My father wanted you to have some start-up money for stock and expenses," she said without pleasure.

"Thank you," I said, to be saying something.

With that, Amy and Fowler put on their coats and turned to leave.

"Hey, Fowler," I said, stopping them. "What are you doing around here?"

"Oh, well, I got married and my wife is from around this area." He looked almost startled that I had started a conversation.

"Things worked out for me in Las Vegas. That seems like forever ago," I said. "Hope all is well."

He nodded and walked out the front door with Amy.

I made sure the door was unlocked so my new customers could come in and I dimmed the lights. When I went around the bar, I turned on the TV and put the channel on ESPN. I went to get myself a beer and realized I should take care of my customers first.

Jerry Number One ordered a Bud, Rocco got a scotch, TC got a B&B, and Jerry Number Two got a cosmopolitan. I went into the cooler and grabbed a Schlitz.

"To AJ," I said, and held up my can of beer.

"Here, here," Rocco said.

Everyone took a sip and the bar got uncharacteristically quiet. I let it hang for a couple of beats before I broke the silence.

"Anyone else feel like they didn't know AJ very well?"

The guys maintained an awkward silence. Jerry Number Two broke it. "How well do any of us really know any of us?"

"Let's not get deep tonight," Rocco said. "AJ wouldn't approve."

That was probably true. AJ would just wince like his stomach bothered him when the guys spoke.

The door opened and my buddy Mike Kelley came in. Since making detective, he'd taken to wearing suit coats, usually the kind you get at Boscovs, along with Dockers and loafers. He'd made detective two years ago, but the outfits still looked out of place.

He had another guy with him, obviously also in law enforcement. Navy blue blazer, blue shirt, red tie, grey slacks, built like a division three college inside linebacker. Dark hair, five-o'clock shadow and a unibrow.

"Duff, this is Agent Kurth. He's temporarily assigned to the area from the D-E-A."

"Nice to meet you," I said. We shook hands and they took their seats at the bar.

"By the way, what are you doing back behind the bar? AJ is gonna kill you," Kelley said.

He hadn't heard.

The room got weird and quiet again.

"AJ died last night," I said, trying to leave out any judgment or awkwardness.

I slid a Bud Light in front of Kelley.

"He left the place to Duffy," Rocco said.

Kelley's eyes shifted from Rocco to me and back again. Kelley seemed to give it some thought.

"How's that going to sit with your addiction-counseling job?" Kelley asked.

I smiled. "I quit this morning," I said.

Kelley squinted and shook his head. "I guess it's been a busy day for you, then," he said.

"Yeah, sort of," I said, trying to muster some nonchalance.

I slid a Bud light in front of Kelley.

"Agent Kurth, what can I get you?"

He scrunched his forehead up like he was having a tough time deciding.

"Ahh, I don't know. I guess I'll have a Bud Light, too."

I took care of him.

"What are you doing in this half-ass town?" I said, to make conversation.

"Mostly, background stuff. Watching how drugs are trafficked up and down the Hudson. Each city from New York to Yonkers, Hudson, and Albany work as a pipeline. Crawford is not a major outpost, but it still is part of the overall system," he said, with just a little of that kind of federal polish.

"Sounds like you'll be looking into the Green Street Gangstars, huh?" The Gangstars, spelled with an "A," were a regional gang, originally from Albany's Green Street. The GSGs controlled the street-level drug trade.

"Of course, they are at the center of it. This new Uzi shit is going to cause an epidemic," Kurth said.

Uzi was a new analog of fentanyl. Some evil genius had found a way to alter a few chemicals in the compound and create a better high that was more addicting. It was also more deadly.

"It's too bad the marketing geniuses behind it didn't apply their smarts to Microsoft or Apple," I said.

"That's for sure," Kurth said. He was only half through his beer.

"I worked in a drug clinic for the last ten years and I can tell you from the clientele that we have it all. Maybe we get it a little later than New York and we're behind them for new things by about six months, but we definitely get their influence."

"I may look to you as a resource, would that be okay with

you?" he asked, and opened his hands like he was presenting something.

"Oh shit, Kurth..." Kelley said.

Kurth looked confused and looked back at Kelley with some exaggerated confusion.

"Mister Duffy, here, sometimes puts himself in situations where he really doesn't belong...you know what I mean," Kelley said and dipped his head and lifted his eyebrows to punctuate his point.

"Ahh...I promise not to invite him to any cartel invasions or SWAT team carry-outs." He smiled and took a sip of his beer.

"Geez, what could go wrong?" Kelley said.

Chapter Six

The next day I went to AJ's right after I fed and walked the dogs. I was getting into the El Dorado when I heard the two of them howling. They didn't do it every day, but they did it enough and it seemed to be amplified by the Airstream's metal. That's when it dawned on me: I now owned AJ's and there was no one to keep me from bringing the dogs in with me as much as I wanted. Well, maybe the health department, but I decided I'd worry about that another time.

I got there around ten, which gave me an hour before I had to open the door. When I unlocked the door, Dimitri was finishing up, putting the bar stools back on the floor.

"Hey D," I said. Al and Agnes walked up quietly to him and he petted them both gently, looking down at them before he made eye contact with me again.

"What's up, Duff? What are you doing here?" The two hounds walked slowly over to the corner in between the bathrooms where AJ had reluctantly left a bed for each of them.

I remembered that Dimitri probably wasn't included in any of the information sharing.

"D, AJ left the place to me," I paused for a second. "I don't know why." I said it as much to myself as to Dimitri.

"So, I still got a job?" Dimitri said.

"Yeah, Man, of course," I said. "Uh, what did he pay you?"

"Fifteen bucks an hour. Two hours a day, six days a week.

Comes to about one-eighty. More if I work more," he said.

I shrugged. "Sounds good to me," and we shook hands. I got a pang in my chest, questioning what the hell I was doing here. Not wanting to say no and not wanting to let the guys down was hardly a reason to become a bar owner. I didn't know what the hell I was going to do.

"You been in the office?" Dimitri asked. I shook my head. He motioned me to the kitchen.

The small office was off the bar and at the opposite end, next to an oversized freezer. Dimitri unlocked it and stood back for me to go inside. I was confused at first and then realized he was being deferential to his boss. This, along with all the other shit, was going to take some getting used to.

There was an old wooden desk in the center of the room. The finish on the top of it was worn and scraped, and on the left side there was a stain that ran down the side of it, suggesting AJ might have spilled a beverage. It was a two-pedestal desk with drawers built into each side. An olive green four-drawer metal file cabinet stood in the corner. The desk had an old-school banker's lamp. It was vintage, not a reproduction.

"You good, Boss?" Dimitri said.

"Yeah." His voice shook me out of my dumbfounded state. "Yeah, Man, thanks." I extended my hand again. Dimitri nodded and headed out.

I sat in the wooden chair behind the desk. It had worn red leather upholstery with an indentation from AJ's ass. Across the top was a framed five-by-seven picture of a young AJ, holding an infant next to what had to be his wife. The couple was full of smiles. It was difficult to recognize AJ because I'm not sure whether I'd ever seen him smile. I felt uncomfortable looking at it.

I pulled open the center drawer and it contained old paperclips, Bic pens without caps, Rolaids and a few old memo-style notepads. The righthand drawer contained a paperback copy of a Gale Sayers biography and three *Sports Illustrated* with Ernie Banks, Ron Santo and other old Cubs on the cover. Interesting,

I never heard AJ mention the Cubs or talk about Wrigley field or anything like that. The lefthand drawer had an address book, one of those business checkbooks and an ashtray from the New York World's Fair.

I opened the big bottom drawer on the left side and there was a stack of Christmas cards, neatly stacked and secured with a thin rubber band. There had to be close to twenty or more of them.

Next to the Christmas cards was a white legal-size envelope with "Duffy" handwritten on it and underlined.

I felt myself swallow and I opened the letter. I began to read.

Duffy,

If you're reading this I'm dead.

I don't mean to be crude about it but I've known for a while that my heart hasn't been too good. You know I'm not a big talker.

I wanted to keep the bar open and you seemed like the best choice. There's a notebook in the file cabinet with as many things as I could remember that you would need to know about the bar. It isn't rocket science but there's some things you gotta know to keep the place open.

I know my daughter would want no part of the place, shit, she's never wanted any part of me. I sent her a letter telling her my plans and she had her lawyer write back to me that she was ok with it. That's just how things have been.

That brings me to the last thing. Over the years I've seen you poke your head into shit that was none of your business. Most of the time I thought you were out of your mind but in the end, I also noticed that shit got done that needed to be done and the little people almost always seemed to turn out all right.

Maybe you could do that for me. I can't tell you more than that because, well, I just can't. I think you'll figure it out as you get experience running this place. Be careful and don't take anything on unless you want to.

Give the dogs a hug for me. Seriously. I never let on, but I always liked seeing them.

AJ

I stared at that letter for a long time. I never had a conversation with AJ much longer than, "Can I have a Schlitz, and can you put the Yankees on?" He winced every time I'd brought Al in, so he did a real good job at concealing his affection for the hound. AJ never really commented about any of my superhero escapades. The most he ever did was shake his head and maybe sneer.

Now, from the grave, a request. For that matter, not an entirely clear request, either. Talk about cryptic.

Be careful.

Don't take anything on unless you want to.

Geez. He was already too late. I took on this bar.

Before I could finish that thought, Al barked and I heard someone respond.

"Hey, Al. Don't get up," It was Jerry Number Two, the first customer of the day. "Good day, Barkeep. Does the health department know about your maître de?"

"What's up, Jer?" I said.

"Whole lot of nothin'," he said.

I poured Jerry his Diet Coke and turned on the TV. It was already on Sports Center. I looked at the back of the bar and decided I should wipe down the bottles or something. I found a rag and rinsed it off.

"Hey, Duff. What's going on?" Jerry said after just a moment.

I stopped wiping and turned to look at Jerry. He had put his newspaper down and was looking intently at me.

"Huh?" I said.

"C'mon, I know you. What's up?" he asked.

Something inside told me not to mention anything about AJ's letter. I didn't know why. It was just an instinct.

"I guess it is just hitting me what's happened in the last few days. AJ, T-J, my job, this place... Lot of changes in a short period of time," I said.

"Everything turned upside down, huh?" Jerry said, folding his paper.

Thankfully the front door opened, and a customer came in. A late fortyish guy, smooth light-brown leather jacket, designer jeans, and slicked-back hair, took the seat at the end of the bar on the corner right before it wrapped around. He had a strange smile on his face.

"Hi, what can I get you?" I asked. Mister Hospitality.

He just looked at me for a long moment.

"Where's AJ?" he asked. No introduction, no conversation.

I looked at him and tried to take him in. Nothing came to me but he didn't feel right.

"Uh, AJ passed away the other night," I said. I tried to be reverent but not too solemn because I had no idea who this guy was.

"Who are you, then?" he asked. He had an attitude about him.

I was starting to not like this guy. I didn't owe him an explanation. It was my place, and he should show me some respect. Maybe he was something to AJ, so he'd get a little bit of the benefit of the doubt.

"Duffy," was all I said.

He smiled again. That creepy smile. "Duffy. You related to AJ?"

I looked at the guy in the eyes. "You know, I didn't get your name," I said. I gave it enough civility that it didn't sound as much like a fuck-you as I had meant it to.

He paused a moment. Then he nodded. "Renzo."

I waited to see if there was going to be anything else. There wasn't.

I said, "No, I'm no relation to AJ. He left me the place. Can I get you something?"

Again, the pause.

"Yeah, Johnny Black, rocks." I turned to make the drink. He had his phone out and was punching numbers. He got up and went out the front door. I put his drink on a coaster in front of his seat. I looked at Jerry.

"Must be the fifth," he said.

"Huh?"

"This guy comes in on the fifth of every month in the middle of the day, sometimes a little more often, and randomly, and never says anything. AJ never charged him," Jerry said.

I let that sink in and before I could respond, Renzo was back inside.

"First one's on the house," I said and smiled, even though I didn't feel like it.

"AJ never charged me," Renzo said with his smile. "For any drinks."

"That so?"

"Yeah," Renzo said. His eyes locked into mine.

"AJ's dead," I said.

Renzo sipped his drink and stared straight ahead. He didn't make eye contact and he didn't make conversation. He wasn't drinking fast enough to be a chronic alcoholic who had to have one in the middle of the day on the fifth when he was traveling.

Oddly, it cast a pall over the bar. Jerry wasn't talking, which was odd.

Renzo's phone rang and he didn't even bother to look. He went outside again.

"Guy's a creep," Jerry Number Two said.

Renzo came back in, sliding the phone into the inside pocket of his jacket. His face had lost expression, but there was something to it that made me feel that he wasn't happy.

"I'll have another," he said, with not even a hint of politeness.

I poured the drink, put a fresh swizzle stick in it and went to put it in front of him.

"Eight dollars," I said.

He glared at me.

"I told you, AJ didn't charge me for drinks," he said.

"Yeah, I heard you. It's eight dollars," I said.

He continued to stare at me. I noticed a scar near his hairline and another one just to the side of his ear.

"You aren't big on tradition?" he said, and smirked.

"Running a business is all," I said, and smiled, but I didn't put any warmth in it.

He reached for the drink and I pulled it away before he could grab it.

"Why don't you find another place to drink," I said. I heard Al and Agnes scritch-scratch their way up from the floor. They sat ten feet away from Renzo and looked at him without blinking. Al started to growl.

"That long-eared mutt keeps it up and he's gonna get a boot," Renzo said.

That did it.

"Now, it is time to get the fuck out," I said. I lifted the hinged part of the bar near the service sink and walked around him. I opened the door. "Get out and don't come back, understand?"

He glared at me, chuckled to himself and made a show of taking his time in getting up. He walked past me slowly and stopped on the threshold.

"You have no idea. You have no fucking idea..." Then he headed to a black Escalade parked across the street.

The dogs were unsettled. Al did the thing where he moves from one paw to the other and Agnes was doing a high pitch wine. I patted them both on the head and got back behind the bar.

I picked up his glass and washed it out. I went back to wiping things down. I could feel my adrenaline pumping a bit more than I wanted to admit. It hadn't come real close to becoming physical but it was close enough. The guy hadn't backed down, and I got the sense he'd be comfortable with a street fight.

I wanted to talk to the guys about some things. I gave it some thought before I asked Jerry.

"What do you know about that guy?" I said.

Jerry put down his newspaper.

"Nothin', really," he said. "Like I told you, he came in on the fifth of the month. AJ gave him free drinks. He sat there for an hour or two and then he left. Once in a while, he'd come in on other days but it was the same routine. He'd sit there, drink for free, and not say nothin'."

"Every month?"

"Yeah," Jerry said. "I don't remember them having any noteworthy conversations."

I gave Jerry another Diet Coke.

"How long has he been coming in?" I asked.

"At least as long as I've been coming here. Maybe 15 years or more," Jerry said.

"And they never spoke?" I found it hard to believe.

Jerry seemed to give it some thought. "He mentioned 'The Old Man' once and he said something about Chicago."

"Something about Chicago? Like what?" I asked.

"I dunno. He might even have said that into his phone. I got the impression AJ didn't like him much," Jerry said.

AJ hadn't liked anyone much. It would have been pretty hard to tell if he didn't like you. I never thought he liked me until he left me this bar. This whole thing, leaving me the bar, the note, and now Renzo, didn't make any sense and it gave me a funny feeling.

Sports Center was going on about LeBron and the configuration of his purchased roster and that noise distracted me enough to interrupt my obsessing. That, and Rocco coming in.

"Good afternoon, Sir," I said.

I poured his Dewar's on the rocks and placed it on a coaster in front of him. I let him get situated before I picked up the same line of questioning.

"Hey Roc, what do ya know about a guy named Renzo, who was just here? Jerry said he used to come in on the fifth of the month, like, for years," I said.

"I passed him coming in. I don't know anything about him. I never heard him ever really say anything. Gave me the creeps. Kind of a squirrel," Rocco said.

"So, he comes in on the fifth of every month, some other

times, drinks for free and says nothing to nobody?" I asked.

The guys both shrugged.

"How was AJ when he came around?"

"You know AJ, he always looked annoyed. Maybe a little more so on Renzo days," Jerry said.

"AJ never said anything to me, but I do remember one time I caught him muttering under his breath. Kept saying 'Sonofa-bitch, sonofabitch...'"

"Why?"

"Who knows?" Rocco said. "It certainly wasn't because they were close friends, reuniting."

"You guys know much about AJ, I mean his past?" I asked.

They both shook their heads. We all seemed a little sheepish about the fact that we didn't know much about a guy we saw every night of our lives.

At least I felt sheepish.

Chapter Seven

Detective Kelley and Agent Kurth came in later that night. Tired and stressed, I skipped any kidding around and just got them their Bud Lights. Kelley and Kurth turned toward the television and ESPN and occasionally murmured something to each other about sports that I didn't entirely pick up. Kelley was three quarters done with his beer before he spoke.

"How's the bar business treating you? I mean, from that viewpoint?" he asked. I got the impression he was just trying to make conversation.

"Been a weird first day," I said.

He drank from the long neck.

"How so?"

I wasn't sure if I wanted to get into the Renzo story. The place was empty except for the three of us, so I figured, what the hell.

"This guy came in today. Called himself, Renzo," I tried to be economical with the words. "Ordered a drink and said AJ never charged him for any drinks. The guys said he came in on the fifth of the month. Never said anything but he always put AJ in a bad mood."

"AJ was always in a bad mood," Kelley said.

"That's what I said. Anyway, I didn't like the guy from the get-go. I told him the first one's free, and he said AJ never charged him. I told him AJ was dead and when he made a crack about giving Al the boot, I threw him out."

"Sensitive history with Al and the boot." Kelley finished his beer, and I opened a fresh one in front of him.

"Yeah, but it was more than that. He was trying to be badass and was acting like I should be intimidated."

"You don't take well to that."

"Never have," I said. I got a beer out of the cooler for myself. "He told me that I had no idea what I was doing. I showed him to the door."

Kelley nodded a few times. "I think you'll see him again."

"I do too."

Kurth just followed along without saying anything. After that exchange, the guys finished up, said good night and headed out.

I closed up a little after one. Best I could tell, the bar took in a little more than two hundred dollars for the day. It dawned on me I had very little idea about actually running a business, stuff like profit and loss and accounting. There was probably stuff about taxes and inventory and all sorts of shit I had no idea about. It left me with an uneasy feeling.

It also made me wonder what the hell I was doing, accepting the bar.

Al and Agnes had spent the day in the bar with me and I sensed they were a bit uneasy, as well. I didn't feel like walking them when I got home but I knew I'd pay the price if I didn't. It was late September and it was in the low fifties, so I didn't really have a good excuse for not walking them. I decided a walk down 9R would be a good idea before bed. Elvis was doing "Come What May," a jazzy, upbeat number from the early sixties. It was a cut no one really talked about, but I liked it a lot.

I rolled down the windows to air out the Cadillac. Driving with Al for years had left the upholstery with a funked-up smell, but adding Agnes, a one-hundred-forty-pound bloodhound to the mix more than doubled the aromatherapy. The night air was cool but also a bit heavy with dampness. I was a mile from my trailer when I noticed the Crawford smell. The city had a smell all of its own, different than the inside of my hound-mobile. I wondered if the First Prize Meats slaughterhouse elevator was on the fritz again. Tonight, the city seemed especially smelly.

As I got closer to home, I realized that wasn't it. The sky had a strange orange cast to it. The last half mile the smell got more intense and when I came around the bend that led to my house, I saw why.

My trailer was engulfed in flames.

I stared in disbelief. There was no temptation to rush in. The flames were thick coming out of the Airstream, which had already begun to melt on one end. They were bluish at the roots and I knew nothing would be salvageable.

I kept the dogs in the car and got out just to look at it. It was way too early to process anything. The sirens began and they got louder and clearer by the second. I had no idea what to do, how to feel or who to reach out to—another thing my brain and soul would struggle to process.

Add it to the list.

The fire trucks pulled in, the men scrambling out of the trucks, hoses, axes, nozzles, yelling and screaming. I took a few steps up my driveway, still a good distance from the Moody Blue, my nickname for my now-former residence. The smell would stick with me forever and the sick feeling in my gut was going to leave its own mark.

That's when I saw it. Right in the middle of my driveway.

Out of place, but in a moment's thought, it made sense. It brought some logic to what was going on in front of me.

In the middle of the dirt driveway sat a quart of Johnny Walker Black.

Chapter Eight

Kelley must've heard the radio call. He was at my place just minutes after the fire engines arrived.

"Jesus, Duff," he said, "the dogs all right?"

"Yeah, they were with me in the car." I was holding the bottle of Johnny Walker.

"Not that it's important right now, but what's with the scotch. Did you make a change?" It was hard to hear him over the sounds of the fire engines pumping water and the men tearing apart what was left of my home with axes.

"It was left in the driveway so I'd find it."

When I looked at Kelley the sirens reflected off his face and cast him in red light.

"I don't get it..."

"That asshole at the bar today. I refused him a free Johnny Walker before I threw him out," I said.

"You know any more about the guy?"

"All I know is his name is 'Renzo.' I know he came to sit in AJ's on the fifth of every month, stopped by once in a while besides that, didn't say anything to anyone and that AJ didn't like him. That's it, like I told you earlier."

Kelley nodded his head a few times and absent-mindedly kicked at the gravel. He looked up at the Moody Blue and winced. The fire was beginning to die down. There still were some flaming spots, but mostly it was just smoldering.

Kelley and I stood without saying anything for a long moment.

The firefighters kept working, kept yelling back and forth and kept expending energy.

I just stared.

Kelley broke the silence. "You wanna stay at my place?" he offered. I knew he would. It didn't matter that I had two smelly and incorrigible hounds. It didn't matter that his wife wasn't my biggest fan. I knew he would.

"Nah, I think it's about time I checked out the apartment AJ had above the bar. It's furnished and, well, I own it, I guess." The words sounded weird coming out of my mouth.

He nodded again, kicked some more gravel and had that look like he wanted to say something but wasn't sure whether he should.

"It doesn't matter what I say," he spoke softly and deliberately. I could make out what he was saying, but just barely. "You're going to, uh..." he didn't finish.

"Yeah, Kell, I am."

"Of course, you are." He paused. "Be careful, will ya?"

I couldn't imagine there'd be anything left in the rubble and the fire chief told me to stay out of it until they cleared it. It would be taped off and protected while they investigated the cause. They'd let me know when I could go through it and, in the meantime, they'd collect any possessions that seemed worth salvaging. I thanked them, took a deep breath and decided to go back to the bar.

Losing my home and just about all of my possessions, as well as my girl, my job, a close friend and my coach in the space of seventy-two hours had left me, I guess, just a tad disoriented.

Maybe a bit more than a "tad." Maybe more like a fucking shitload.

The bar had two floors above it. I never had been up there,

nor did I ever hear what it was used for. AJ wasn't a real talkative guy and I had never given much thought to the space above the place I spent so much time in. With the two hounds in tow, I flipped the light switch and went up the back stairs that were just outside AJ's... I mean, my...office.

The light was dim light and both Al and Agnes hesitated. Al's short legs didn't work great on the short stairs and Agnes was a bit of a scaredy-dog anyway, so she started to whine. The door had a skeleton key in the lock and before I turned it, I took a deep breath, not knowing what I was about to find.

The first thing that hit me was the musty smell of a place that hadn't been exposed to any fresh air in a long time. I flipped on the light and as my eyes adjusted to it, I took in the front room. It was a living room with a leather couch and loveseat, two end tables with lamps and an area rug on top of a hardwood floor. On a stand across from the couch was an old console-type television, the kind where the cabinet looked like furniture. It matched the coffee table and end tables.

There was a doorway that led into a kitchen. It was a galley kitchen, long and slim with an old but functioning refrigerator, as I could hear it running. The sink was that sixties avocado green, but when I turned on the faucet, water came out. When I opened the cabinets and drawers there was a matching set of dishes and silverware.

The bedroom had a neatly made, full-size bed, a dresser and a closet. The closet had a few boxes in it, and there was a mirror over the dresser. There was an envelope tucked into the mirror's frame. It wasn't sealed.

Duff,

This apartment goes along with the bar. It's yours to rent or live in.

I've always wondered how you lived in that trailer. Hope this could be an alternative or a source of income.

Thanks for looking into that thing for me.

AJ

I read it over again. I was confused. I'd never really thought I meant that much to AJ, yet now he was treating me like a long, lost son. It also made me wonder about his death. He seemed to be very prepared and he left things behind organized. Did he know he was about to die?

And he really, really wanted me to solve his problem, whatever it was. And why hadn't he just come out and told me?

Did he know I was about to lose my trailer? How could he have known that?

I opened up the top drawer and what I actually saw made me step back.

It was a handgun. There was a sticky note on the handle.

I know you're not a big fan of these but it might be a good idea to carry this for a while. It isn't licensed so be careful with it. If, or shit, when, you start finding out what happened some people may not be thrilled. Please be careful.

You can let Al sleep on the bed. I'm not around anymore to get annoyed.

AJ

What the hell had I gotten myself into?

Chapter Nine

There wasn't much sleep to be had that night. Al didn't accept his new digs—he was a real creature of habit—and Agnes just never relaxed. I was up about every thirty minutes or so and I discovered living on a second-floor complicated life with animals. It now meant a walk down a flight of stairs to let the dogs out, whereas before it had meant simply opening a sliding door.

I'm all for embracing change but there seemed to be an awful lot to wrap my arms around lately.

It also dawned on me that I was now living a minimalist life, not because of the teachings of some self-help guru but because all of my shit was gone. The extra money AJ had left for me was going to have to go for more things than stocking beers and cleaning supplies. I didn't want this as a career, but I didn't have a alternative at present.

In the morning, I planned on making a shopping trip but before I could get out the door my phone rang.

It was Shony. About fifteen years ago I got her out of a sick white slavery porn thing that she got kidnapped into.

"Duffy, oh my God, are you okay?" She was panicked.

"Shony, easy kid, I'm fine. Trailer is gone and everything in it but me, Al and Agnes. We're all one-hundred percent okay." I tried to be as calm as I could. In my present state it took some effort.

"Oh, thank Jesus!"

"Believe me, I have," I said. "Tell me, how's the gig?" Shony was working with foster kids.

"Oh Duff, I love it! It feels so good to give back." I could hear the excitement in her voice.

"And your step-brother Raheen? He okay? I'll never forget when he showed up to help me out. Said it was because of you. That was really something." Raheen and his two associates helped me out when I needed some muscle. Kid said he owed me because I saved his sister.

"We don't speak. I told him I loved him but he's living that gang lifestyle and I had to let him go," she said. Her voice had turned somber and I was sorry I'd brought it up.

"That's too bad." It was all I could think of to say.

"I prayed on it and I'm at peace. I'm hoping he'll see the light."

"I'll pray, too. In the meantime, you come see me. I'm now a bar owner."

"What?"

"I'll explain. Just come down to AJ's some afternoon and we will catch up," I said. After that we signed off. It was great to hear from her and it took me away from some of the other stuff that was going on.

I made a trip to Walmart to get some bare essentials. After that, I was in the bar by eleven o'clock and tried to do the things that I thought a bar owner should do. I wiped down the bar, I checked the coolers for inventory, and I made sure the draft lines were cleared. I put the TV on ESPN and learned that Tom Brady was great…again. Mentally, I reminded myself that Joe Montana never lost a Super Bowl, while the GOAT had lost three.

Rocco came in just after noon and ordered the first drink of the day. Scotch at midday was fine for a retired guy, and he'd nurse it throughout the afternoon. Rocco didn't come in every day in the afternoon, he was part of the nighttime shift, mostly, but he'd do some day drinking from time to time.

"I heard about the fire," Rocco said. His face was tight, and he made eye contact with me. "They have any idea what happened?"

"I got a pretty good idea," I said, trying not to be dramatic.

"Yeah, what?" Rocco said.

"That guy, Renzo, you know the creep that came in yesterday?"

"Really? I mean, Duff, I think he's a creep, too, but isn't it kind of a leap to think he'd burn down your house?"

"There was a bottle of Johnny Walker left in my driveway. It was pretty clear it was meant for me to find it. I don't drink Scotch." I wiped down some glasses that were already clean to be doing something. Having to say out loud what Renzo had done seemed to make it more real. I could feel it build up inside of me.

"Son of a bitch..." Rocco said.

"Yeah." I agreed.

"What the hell are you gonna do?" Rocco asked after pausing for a moment to think things over.

I shrugged. "What else is there to do? You gotta get up in the morning, right?"

"Where you stayin'?"

"Upstairs. There's an apartment upstairs. It is furnished. Like AJ was getting ready to rent it out or something. You ever been up there?" He had barely touched his drink. It was like a prop that gave him just enough reason to be in the bar.

"I was up there a month ago. There was no apartment," Rocco said with just a trace of Roccoian annoyance.

"What? I stayed there last night. It was one-hundred-percent furnished. Like AJ was going to have a tenant or something," I said.

"There were a half dozen broken and dusty bar stools when I was there. An old cash register, a bunch of empty cardboard beer cases and a broken TV," Rocco said.

We were both quiet for a moment. ESPN droned on in the background.

"Did he mention anything to you about renovating it?" I asked.

"No, nothing," Rocco gave it some thought. "It's almost like he knew...knew...I don't know..." He let it trail off.

"That he was going to die?" I asked, saying what Rocco wouldn't.

"Yeah..." Rocco almost whispered under his breath.

"People don't know they're going to have a heart attack," I said.

"Are we sure that's what it was?" Rocco said.

"I just assumed..." The front door opened and interrupted our conversation.

"Kyrone, what are you doing here?" Kyrone was one of my clients from the clinic. I looked at my watch. "You're supposed to be in group right now."

It was a quarter past two and his addiction group therapy session back at the clinic had started at two. He pulled out the stool at the end of the bar closest to the front door. He didn't say anything. I walked toward him, but he kept quiet for the longest time. He was twenty-eight, a former high school basketball standout at Crawford High. Even though he was only five-seven, he could dunk like it was nothing. He screwed up a college scholarship and wound up on heroin after he blew out his knee. Kyrone looked like the guy who played Martin Sheen's personal assistant on West Wing.

When he was on my caseload, he hadn't talked much, and I always questioned his motivation.

"You just left," he said. I wasn't sure I'd heard him right. "You just left."

I felt a pang of guilt shoot through me. It caused my stomach to sicken.

He just let it hang there. I didn't know what to say. His eyes welled.

I swallowed hard. I felt shame. I had blown out of the clinic filled with rage and hatred for the years of dealing with Claudia. I worried about my income, I worried about the change in my life and I worried about making a hard decision. It had only been a couple of days but I hadn't yet gotten around to worrying about the caseload I'd left behind.

I was ashamed.

"I don't know what to say. I got really pissed about something on the job, something that had been going on for years, but, uh, now I see that just blowing out of there wasn't right. It wasn't fair," I said.

Kyrone looked away, staring at the wall without any real focus. It got quiet, except for the TV, which Rocco had changed to Bonanza.

"You got coffee?" he asked. It sounded strange.

"Yeah, how do you take it?" I asked. I didn't know what else to say. He was on my caseload and a social relationship with him went against counselor ethics.

Except I wasn't a counselor anymore.

"Four sugars, lots of cream."

Sounded like an addict's coffee choice. A little bit of anything never worked. I got him the coffee and slid it in front of him.

"You told me that opioids fuck with the natural ability to deal with pain."

"Yeah." I vaguely remembered the conversation. It was the typical introductory education I did in a session when someone was new to counseling. Therapy was partly airing feelings, but it was also partly education and helping folks see just what they were up against. I had done it so long I didn't give it much thought anymore.

"Does that, like, apply to emotions pain? I mean, I'm nervous as hell and the littlest things bum me out awful." Kyrone wasn't educated and his syntax was often messed up but there was no denying his innate intelligence.

I gave his point a little thought before I answered.

"Yeah, think about it. You take something that numbs you out and that's how you get used to dealing with things. When that goes away, you're left without your main way to cope. It hurts more and you don't have the skills to deal."

It sounded good to me.

He looked at his coffee and thought about it.

"How long until I'm normal again and don't feel like this all the time?"

I thought about it.

"Uh, tough to say. The thing is, everyone feels pain. Life is kind of about pain. The trick is trying to live with the day-to-day pain enough to let the infrequent bits of happiness shine through." I looked at him to see if he was buying it. "Everyone—everyone who's honest and in touch—is walking around in pain. Its why people get high or drink or do all the other shit to avoid it."

"So, getting high was just kind of rentin' some relief. It was always gonna make it worse."

"That, in a nutshell, is addiction," I said and nodded.

"So, the doctors who prescribe the shit don't know this? Why the fuck did they put me on Oxy when I asked for it? Didn't they know it was gonna fuck me up in the long run?"

Talk about tough questions.

"Doctors treat symptoms. You said you were in pain. You said you wanted Oxy. They don't go much beyond that."

"Is it that or are they into making money? Like, they see easy money and me havin' to come back to get the shit so they can cash in. Don't them doctors have enough already?"

I wasn't sure what to say about that. "Man, I don't know. Maybe there are some like that, maybe some are just too busy and maybe some are stupid. They are people like everyone else," I said.

"Man, I'm hurtin' so much sometimes I don't know what to do. That shit is scary."

He got quiet.

"Can I get more coffee?"

I gave him a refill.

He took a sip and looked like he was going to say something, but he wasn't sure whether he really wanted to.

"Duffy, you don't restrict who comes in here, right? Like

that would be illegal or somethin' right?"

"It's my business. I can't not let people in for their race, religion and shit like that."

I didn't know what he was getting at.

"So, I can come in here when I want..."

I looked him in the eyes, gave it some thought and took a second to respond.

"Sure," I said. I couldn't think of anything else.

"You ever charge for coffee?" He smiled.

"Nah, it's on the house."

Kyrone smiled and left.

It wasn't long after that when I got another surprise.

The door opened and in walked my ol' buddy Pasquale. Most people called him "Squal" and he was a bouncer of some significance at The Taco, the strip joint where TJ, my, uh, sort-of ex, worked. The guy was the quintessential professional who could work a door like no other.

It didn't hurt that he weighed about two-seventy-five and had the build of a former defensive lineman. That's not unique—that's de rigueur for the field. What made "The Squal" different was that he knew how to work the door. He could talk any drunk idiot down and make him like the fact that he was being thrown out. He could give a bunch of college sophomores a look that would bring the ruckus down thirty-five percent on the obnoxious meter and he could intervene in a lover's quarrel better than Dr. Phil.

And when somebody needed to be thrown out...shit.

I've known him long enough to know he was good with his hands. He could deflect, parry and counter faster than Hector Camacho but it seldom came to that. Squal may not have been in varsity shape anymore, but he had the muscle memory. If a guy, or actually a group of guys were trouble, he would lower his center of gravity and drive forward like something between

Lawrence Taylor and Haystack Calhoun.

And he'd appreciate the wrestling reference.

"Duffy! A bar owner! What the hell?!" he said with his big smile, spreading his arms wide for a bro-hug.

"Yeah, what the hell is right!" I said.

"Sorry to hear about AJ..."

I nodded. There was the requisite silence of reverence.

"What the hell are you doing here?"

"I caught wind of you taking over and I wanted to pay tribute."

"Man, that's nice." I gave it a second. "Narragansett?"

He was the only guy I knew who drank a beer worse than Schlitz.

"Duff, you're the best!" I slid one of the foulest-tasting beers I'd ever tasted in front of him. I was a hero and...I didn't have to drink the stuff.

Squal put down three-quarters of the can in a gulp, semi-burped, exhaled and smiled.

"That's good shit." He waited a beat. "How's T-J?"

I felt it in my gut and then felt the awkward thing about how to respond.

I just shook my head.

"Aw, Duff, Sorry..."

"All good." I changed the subject quickly. "What's up at The Taco?"

"You know, tits and ass...no offense...T-J and all..."

I waved him off.

"Anything else going on?" I said to sort of smooth the transition.

"Yeah, I was on *Jeopardy!*"

That just hung there. Rocco, a *Jeopardy!* aficionado, whipped his head around.

"What?" I said.

"Yeah, lifelong dream. I applied, won the audition and went on."

"How'd you do?" I said, kinda feeling like I was in another universe.

"Can't say. Contractually obligated. I'm on next Monday."

"Holy crap!" I said. "Hey, don't take this the wrong way but, uh..."

He interrupted me.

"I know Duff, folks don't picture a thug like me being a brainiac. I didn't set out to be a strip-club bouncer. I gotta English degree. Just never put it to work," he said. There wasn't a shred of being offended.

"And still working the door, how's that going?" I shook my head.

"The same. You know; what is there to be different? The new owner is cool. She treats the girls better and there's no bullshit."

I opened another Narragansett and slid it in front of him. I was quiet for just about a beat too long.

"What the hell happened to you and T-J?"

"We're kind of done. She sort of disappeared," I said, trying to be honest with turning a nice visit awkward.

"Again?" Squal said. The realization that this has happened before cut into me.

I shrugged.

"What are you going to do?"

"I guess I'm a little sick of the back and forth, the go away, come closer. I mean, she's got stuff to figure out," I said.

I was lapsing into too much explaining. I changed the subject.

Squal, let me ask you something."

"Sure."

"You ever run into a guy named Renzo? Early forties, big, broken nose, leather suit jacket type. Kind of acts like he wanted to be on *The Sopranos* or something."

"That asshole? Yeah, I know him." Squal looked like he'd eaten some bad eggs. "The fucking guy comes in once a month, always on the fifth. Rude to the dancers, tries to buddy up to me. Thinks he's a badass."

"What's his deal?'

"Says he's from Chicago, talks about checking on some accounts. Always real cryptic in that way that is supposed to fascinate and intimidate you. Tries to see if I want to buy in to one of his 'operations' without ever detailing what his 'operations' are. I don't buy into it and start talking about the N-F-L. He always seems a little disappointed that I'm not asking him a bunch of questions."

"Any idea about his accounts?"

"No, but the implication is that he's collecting for bets or loan-sharking or some bullshit. He tries to pull that vibe off. He's right from central casting with the leather, gold chain and dropping the g's off his gerunds."

"You really do have an English degree..."

He laughed at that.

"Why do you want to know?" He took another gulp of that horrid beer.

"He came in here. It was the fifth. Told me AJ always gave him free drinks. Asked if I was related to AJ and if I owned the joint. He said some shit to Al, and I threw him out. That night my trailer was burned down."

"Motherfucker..."

"Yeah. The guys said he would come once a month and AJ would give him free drinks and he would just sit there. AJ never explained it to anyone."

"That's weird. He doesn't do business with anyone at The Taco. I get the impression he comes in at the end of his day. He's one of these dudes whose only relationship with women is as hookers and strippers. Perpetual antisocial permanent adolescent."

"I'll take psychology for eight hundred dollars, Alex," I said.

Squal smiled. "Look Duff, I gotta get back there. Just wanted to congratulate you on the place. I'll keep my eye out for the douche-bag and let you know if I find out anything."

"Thanks, I appreciate that," I said. We bumped fists and he split.

Chapter Ten

I tried calling Amy, AJ's daughter, but it went straight to voicemail. I tried three times and she never picked up. I'm guessing she had my name in her contacts and just didn't feel like talking to me.

I had no kids and sometimes I felt a little sad about that. I had thought about raising a boy, try to impart my values, teach him to throw a ball, maybe box, watch him become a teenager and then a man. Late in life he could come over for Sunday dinner and we'd share a cigar or a fine bourbon and watch a football game we didn't care about.

He'd ask for advice on his career, the woman he wanted to marry and how he should grow into adulthood.

Yeah, right.

Or, I could have a kid who shot heroin, hated me, moved to Alaska to work in a fishery to get away from me and blame me for all his dysfunction. I wasn't exactly crushing life in the area of love relationships, career choices and getting by in general. I had it down to eighty-twenty that my kid would be a fucked-up mess and it would be just another thing that would make my life a shit sandwich.

So, thinking about AJ, I'm sure he had the same feelings. He must've fallen in love, had the joy and hopeful rush of what having a daughter would be like and the promise of the life laid out in front of him.

Then he winds up estranged, working in a dive bar, listening to the bullshit spouted by the same five or six guys every day. It had to be an existential nightmare for him, and as I think back on it, probably explains his perpetual foul mood. The guy always looked like he had agita.

His daughter made it clear she hated him and seemed kind of glad he was dead. I thought about that superimposed on my own dreams of parenthood. Yeah, two disobedient hound dogs in a smelly trailer and now in an upstairs apartment, may be void of any grandiosity, but it seemed to be a little less in the kick-in-the-balls department.

Squal mentioned that Renzo was from Chicago. I'm glad he confirmed the Renzo assholism. I trust my instincts about people fairly well, but it was nice to have validation from another male I respected.

Chicago meant one thing for me, Jack Daniels.

I meant the retired detective, not the bourbon. I drink Beam.

I got to know Jack about a decade ago when I got called to a fight in Chicago. Some bastard stole Al, scared me to death and, between Jack and I, we rescued Al. We got the bad guy who, thanks to Al's lack of cooperation, was now missing four fingers on his throwing hand. A beautiful little girl with Down Syndrome had been kidnapped with Al, and she was one-hundred-percent okay and seemed not to be traumatized. I think she had the time of her life with her new short-legged best friend.

I keyed in Jack's cell.

"Daniels," she said, like every detective in every cop show I have ever seen on television.

"Man, Jack, don't you ever soften?" I asked. It was our usual back and forth.

"Must be Duffy. You're the only one who worries about my level of sentimentality. What favor are you looking for now?"

"Geez, Jack, can't one old friend call another?"

"Of course, they can. But you don't. What favor are you looking for? I'm trying to enjoy retirement. I don't know if you heard." It was all sarcasm.

I explained AJ's death, the note, the bar, the fire and the gun. She seemed to be listening. Then I told her about Renzo.

"Once again you're sticking your nose where it doesn't belong."

"Well, sort of..."

There was a pause.

"Okay, there's no use in dissuading you to not be a moron, so let's get to it."

I smiled. "Aww, Jack, you so get me," I affected a Generation-Y accent.

"First of all, I'd be very careful. Sounds like your buddy owed someone something. If this Renzo is from Chicago and he comes to visit your guy every fifth for seventeen years then something important occurred. That's a lot of effort to expend over a bunch of years."

"True," I said, to let her know I was listening.

"Second, this is the city with the broad shoulders, and the chance that this has something to do with organized crime seems pretty evident."

"Okay..."

"What fuckin' cow town do you live in, again?" she asked.

"I beg your pardon? I live in Crawford, about an hour from New York City."

"Yeah, spare me the civic pride. How close are you to Schenectady?"

That surprised me.

"Not far, maybe an eighty-minute drive up the thruway? That's weird, that's where AJ was living before he moved here."

"Schenectady is, or at least used to be, a mob town run by some of our friends here in Chicago." She was on a bit of a roll.

"Why would the Chicago Mafia care about Schenectady?"

"For the same reason MacDonald's expanded from San Diego. Wise guys start up in a city and they need protection or a place to cover their bets. When they get big enough, they have to find people with deeper pockets and more influence."

"So, Schenectady is part of the Chicago mob?"

"Let me guess. Let's see, I'm betting Schenectady is known for more bookies, street hookers and shady business deals than say, Albany or Troy, or the other cities close by...right?"

"Yeah, now that I think about it, yeah."

"Bet they have porn shops, or at least used to, before it all became wonderfully free on the Internet?"

"Yeah..."

"That's organized crime, my friend. The politicians, the judges, the police have to look the other way, at least a little, for that stuff to be going on. It isn't huge, but it is there."

"Okay, what about a guy named, Renzo, what do you know about him?" I asked.

She laughed. "There are maybe five million people in this city. There's a huge organized crime faction—not all Italian-Americans, by the way—but political correctness aside, a fair number of them go by "Renzo."'

"Can you try to find out about a guy named Renzo who might have a reason to come east?"

She sighed, hard.

"Oh sure, Duff. In my free time here in Chicago. I'll look into it because it's not like I wanted to leave law enforcement behind."

"You're the best, Jack. I owe you a beer."

"Uh-huh, still waiting on that last one I believe."

I laughed. "I pay my bets! Don't worry I won't Welsh on it."

"Yeah, right," She sort of laughed or maybe more accurately sighed. "Goodbye, Duffy."

The bar was empty by mid-afternoon and I was thinking about all the things I wanted to do. I needed to talk to AJ's daughter somehow; I wanted to find out about her father before there was an AJ's, and I wanted to find out about what he did with his time and how he came to move his entire life and career to Crawford. Why did he leave his family behind? What the hell happened?

I also could use some time to do some things like, oh, say, replace all my personal items.

I needed a staff.

Dimitri could probably man the bar in a crunch, but he had a little boy he was bringing up on his own and it didn't feel right to mess with that. I didn't have many friends, and the ones I had were usually fighters who wouldn't necessarily bring the required skill set to the hospitality business. The other people I knew were already in the bar business.

Two people came to mind: Billy and Trina. Billy was a guy I'd met when he was a goofy karate-obsessed kid without a dad and a frazzled mom. I helped them out and, I think this is important to note, Billy wound up saving my life. Since then, the guy has grown into an MMA beast who has the respect of the gym. He was going to school to get his master's in social work and was working part time with special-needs kids and adults.

He could probably use some extra money. I gave him a call.

"Duff, what's up?" he said, by way of greeting. "What the hell happened to Smitty?"

I filled him in on Smitty's family stuff.

"I was there yesterday, and the gym has a different feel. It's a little like the wild west," he said.

"What do you mean?"

"There's no one in charge. There's loud Rap music, people aren't following the rules. No one's picking up the place."

"That's a shame."

"I heard they wanted you to take over. You gonna?"

I hesitated. "I don't think so, Billy. I don't want the responsibility."

"But Duff, the place is going to go down the drain. Somebody's gotta step up."

I hesitated again. "I need a workout soon. I'll come down and get a sense of it, but Man, I'm no Smitty.

"All right," he said, to finish off the thread of the conversation. "What else is up?"

I told him about the bar and my job.

"You wanna come work for me?" I asked a little sheepishly. "I'm not sure how long I'm gonna be in business. To be honest this shit fell in my lap and I don't think it's for me. Still, I could use the help."

"Shit, Duff, I don't know anything about the bar business or bartending. I don't even drink that much."

"C'mon down. I'll put you through the AJ's orientation."

He laughed and agreed to come down and check things out. Billy was the closest thing I had to a son. He was more like a mentee, but he was important to me and I was important to him.

It made me feel good.

The guys came in in the early evening.

"That's why they put that stuff in the pool. To catch the kids pissing." Rocco was off and running on swimming pools and urine.

"Little pissers. I think you got a little pisser, Rock," Jerry Number One said.

"If they put it in the water and urine is released, the pool turns bright orange," Rocco said with more certainty than I had for anything in my life."

"Red," Jerry Number Two said.

"I don't remember if I read it or saw it on the Discovery channel," Rocco said.

"No, the pool turns red, not orange," Jerry Number Two.

"How does that even help? I mean aren't all the kids peeing in the pool all the time. I do," TC said.

"It forms a viscous cloud of orange that surrounds the little pisser." Rocco said.

"No need to get vicious. They're just little pissers," TC said.

I decided to interrupt for several reasons.

"Any of you guys remember anything about AJ's before he opened this place?" I asked when they were all there.

"What ya mean? We didn't know each other before this place,"

TC said, stating the obvious. TC held a black belt in stating the obvious.

"He wasn't exactly the most talkative guy, Duff," Jerry Number One said. "Since he died, I've been trying to think of some long, or at least longer, conversations that I had with him. I remember once talking about my family and he said something about family being nothing but hurt."

"What did he mean by that?" Rocco entered the conversation.

"I got the impression it was just that he didn't have a good experience with his," Jerry Number One said.

"After meeting his daughter the other night, I think I understand," Jerry Number Two said. "Didn't get a whole lot of warm and fuzzies from her."

"Who knows?" TC said. "There was probably a divorce and the kid spent her life listening to AJ's wife bad-mouth him."

"Kinda sad, the whole thing," I said.

"One thing that was always odd to me was that one time he got involved in *Jeopardy!*" Jerry Number Two said.

"What are you talking about?" Rocco said with his requisite annoyance.

"You were here. Every night we'd sit and play along with *Jeopardy!* Usually, we ain't real good, but there was a night he aced an entire row and got the double *Jeopardy!* answer," Jerry Number Two said.

"Question." Jerry Number One said.

"Huh?" Rocco asked and made a face.

"On *Jeopardy!* they don't ask questions, they give answers and you have to come up with the question."

"What is 'Go fuck yourself,' Jerry," Rocco said.

"Correct!" Jerry Number Two said. "What the hell were the questions about?"

"You mean answers," TC said.

"Candy." Jerry Number One said.

"That's it!" Jerry Number Two said. "It was like 'Candy

Through History' or something."

"I remember now. He went down the whole column. I asked what was up and he said he used to work for a candy distributor," Rocco said and was quite pleased with himself.

"There you go, Duff. He worked in candy distribution," Jerry Number One said.

I nodded. Great, leave it to the foursome to paint the perfect picture of a man.

Chapter Eleven

I decided to just drop by AJ's daughter's place. If she was going to ignore me, at least this time she'd have to do it to my face. I wasn't even sure what I was going to ask her but I needed to find out more about AJ Part of that was because of the note, the gun and the mystery, but another part of it was something a little bit different.

It bothered me that I hadn't known the man. I saw him damn near every night for more than a decade and a half. He served me beer and occasionally joined in on some of the inanity at the bar, but I realize now, I hadn't known him.

The fact that he left me his place and entrusted me with the task of figuring things out weighed on me. Clearly, he valued our relationship, whatever that relationship was. Maybe he always wanted more from me or maybe the way we were was as capable as he was to befriend another person. I didn't want the bar.

I wondered how many of the people I encountered every day were feeling like this. The quiet desperation, as someone famous once said. The sickness of the human condition, or something.

She lived outside of Schenectady on a lake in a small town called Galway. It was half an hour outside of downtown Schenectady, so I had a ride ahead of me. It may have been a total waste of two hours, but I didn't know what else to do.

It got rural outside Schenectady pretty fast, and you could

tell that by the spaces of land around the houses, but you could also tell it by the political signs on the lawns. People who think New York is a blue state haven't taken a ride outside of the capital area. It gets a lot more like Ohio than New York City pretty fast.

I turned into Weiss Grove, heading down a narrow, one-lane street. I pulled into what looked like a softball field and got a glimpse of the lake through the trees. I could see why someone would want to live here, especially if Schenectady was the other obvious choice.

A sign constructed of stained two-by-fours was near the entrance to the softball field. On it were notices to clean up after your dog, restrictions about what you could put in the dumpsters, and a message about non-residents using the lake. On the other side of the sign was a directory. Her house was in the third row, three in from the lake.

As I got closer, I noticed she was on the side of her house raking leaves. She had rubber boots that covered her calves, a green-and-black-checked flannel shirt and bright yellow work gloves. She looked at me with curiosity as I approached until she recognized me. She winced.

"Hi," I said, as non-threateningly as I could.

"What do you want? What are you doing up here?"

I paused for a second and thought about what I wanted to say.

"Uh, look, I'm not sure what went on with you and your dad—" she interrupted.

"He wasn't my 'dad.' He was my biological father, that's all."

Great job warming her up, I thought.

"Okay, if you could put yourself in my shoes for a moment. I got left the bar and I have no idea why. You see, it is a little embarrassing to say, but though I saw your da...uh...father frequently, I can't say I really knew him very well. I feel bad about that."

"That's too bad." There was a bit more than a little sarcasm in it.

"Can you give me any idea how it came to be or why he picked me?" I asked.

"No, I can't. It was done through the lawyer, Fowler. I was chosen to execute it, but I had nothing to do with it. It makes perfect sense in that he ran out on my mother and me and then stuck us with all the shit to take care of."

"Your mother, is she—"

"She died five years ago. Your friend, the bartender, didn't even send a card."

The picture of AJ wasn't exactly warming.

"Can you tell me anything at all about your father?" I got right to the point. Her hatred was starting to feel like a poison that I wanted to get away from.

"He worked for a candy distributor. His territory was this region down to around where you're from and out to Syracuse. He supplied candy stores, grocery stores, drug stores...stuff like that. Apparently, after a while he quit, left us and bought that dive bar an hour and half away."

"Anything else?"

"I never met the man. My mom didn't exactly fill the house with photographs so she could remember the good times. She wound up working at a grocery store to support us. It was a beautiful way to grow up, trust me." She started to rake again.

"Uh, what about..." I didn't get to finish.

"What about you getting the hell out of here. I don't need this. Go talk to Fowler if you want to know about your friend."

She put all her anger into raking and turned her back to me.

I left without saying goodbye.

On the way out, I got stopped by a guy weed whacking his hedges. He was at the house on the corner and his grey pit bull was at his side. All of a sudden the weed whacker made an awful screeching sound, sputtered and then died.

"God damn thing!" He shouted. I don't think he even knew I

was there. He had white hair, a deep tan, hands that looked like he'd worked his whole life, and a bit of a gut that strained his belt.

"Power tools, Man, what a pain in the ass," I said, to be saying something. "Always seem to be breaking at the wrong time."

"I shouldn't have loaned it to that asshole down the road. Guy could screw up a wet dream," he said. "Never lend out your tools."

He stopped for a second.

"Who the hell are you?" he said. He stopped obsessing over his dysfunctional weed whacker.

"Name's Duffy. I was visiting Amy."

"Oh, what a treat for you. What a bitch." He rolled his eyes. "Big shot from Chicago thinks her shit don't stink. Her old man bought the camp. Now, he was a decent guy."

"AJ?"

"AJ? The guy I knew was Arnold."

"Yeah, that's him." This was getting interesting.

"Used to call him The Candy Man. Worked as a candy salesman and used to give away his samples around the grove in the summer. Good guy."

"What happened to him?" I asked.

"One year he just didn't come up in the summer. No one came. I tried calling. Nothing." He looked in the direction of Amy's house. "It just sat there until Little Miss Sunshine started coming up here three years ago. She paid one of the local guys to fix it up for her. Threw out all of Arnold's stuff."

"Who did the work?" I asked.

"Harry up the road." He paused for a second then yelled "Harry!" It was loud enough that it startled me. "Harry!" he yelled even louder this time. "He'll be down in his golf cart in a second. What did you say your name was?" he extended a hand.

"Duffy."

"I'm Dan. I'm the grove president."

A guy in a souped-up golf cart pulled up. He had on an Irish cap, glasses, and a grey goatee. Big guy, looked like he knew how to handle himself.

"Duffy here, wants to know about ol' Arnold."

"What about him?" Harold said.

"He died and left me his bar. I'd just like to know more about him."

Harry and Dan looked at each other.

"The camp was neat but musty. I had to repair the water lines and Amy wanted me to paint over the old paneling. It wasn't unlike other camps here. People move away and forget about it."

"Did you know anything about his work?" I asked.

"Well, there was a file cabinet filled with paperwork. I tossed it but I remember he was in charge of Schenectady accounts. A mom-and-pop grocery, the Mack pharmacy, and the Sunoco station. Other than that, there were invoices, stuff on Syracuse and Kingston accounts, but I don't remember nothing about that."

"Anything unusual about his stuff or his place?" I asked.

"Like what?" Harry said.

"I don't know. Anything stick out?"

"He had a lot of stuff about the Cubs around but he was from Chicago so that wasn't weird or anything."

I didn't know what else to ask. The three of us stood there for an awkward moment.

"Weren't you the boxer?" Harry asked. "From downstate?"

"Yeah, yeah, that's me," I said. I felt kind of proud to be recognized.

"I saw you get knocked out at the Altamont Fair that time," Harry said.

So much for pride.

I thanked them and headed out.

Chapter Twelve

I headed back to Crawford.

I needed to burn off some uneasiness. I would try to find out more about AJ later but I knew I'd be better off if I got a workout in first. Jumping rope, hitting some bags and the zen of shadow-boxing calmed me and sharpened my focus.

It was going to be my first trip to the gym with no Smitty. Smitty had taken days off, gone on trips and seen to his family down south before, but this would be my first visit where he wasn't the force behind the gym.

He had been the guiding influence behind the gym. The gym wasn't that great when it came to equipment or amenities. The bags were old-school leather and soft in the middle from the years of bodywork, so they were wrapped in duct tape, which, in turn, had become tattered. It had been a continual process to keep them together. That was a principle I could relate to.

There were three speed bags, also beat up, and in Smitty's office there was a stock of bladders that went inside of them to keep them firm. There was the oversized bag to help new guys learn the rhythm and cadence, the medium-sized one for intermediate guys, and the tiniest one for old-school boxers who had been hitting them for years.

The ring's ropes were frayed, and if you leaned into them wrong and your shirt was drenched in sweat you could get a rope burn. The canvas mat that made up the ring floor was originally white but was now dark gray with brown and red stains. The brown dots were faded blood stains and the crimson ones were the newest and freshest marks. The spectrum of red to brown filled out the square and made a collage of bloodshed from years of guys.

The walls were moldy and the odds and ends of weights and barbells provided their resistance without any chrome, logos, or rubber hand grips. The place wasn't funded by any promoters or managers and there were no dues except for the general Y dues, so unless someone brought in some equipment and left it in the gym for others to use, there was never gonna be any new stock of workout gear.

Smitty had kept his few personal items in his office, mostly as souvenirs of his own career. It meant a lot to me that he had bestowed them on me. I just couldn't see myself putting on his headgear and sparring gloves, mostly because I saw them as sacred and a little bit because my own gear was more modern and a little bit better protection-wise.

Smitty's headgear was a Ben-lee and the gloves were old Everlasts. The Ben-lee was the style of headgear that covered the very top of the forehead, the ears and the side of the head. it didn't have the cheek protectors that modern gear had. Cheek protectors protrude far enough to give some protection to the nose, though if you took a good look at me, you could tell by my schnoz that it didn't provide comprehensive coverage. Smitty's left most of your face exposed, which was great for vision, but I like a little bit more coverage for sparring.

His gloves were filled with horsehide, which made it easy to push the filling around and get less padding on the knuckles. That was a shitty thing to do to a training partner, but I had a guy down in Brooklyn do it to me once. I went home from that session with four different cuts, even though I had headgear on and I wound up with twenty stitches. The thumbs weren't attached as they are now. It was around the time that Sugar Ray Leonard developed a detached retina that manufacturers started attaching the thumb to the side of the main mitten of the glove.

It didn't take long to tell Smitty was no longer in the gym. As I came down the stairs to the gym—and way before I made it to the threshold of the door to the gym—I could tell something was different. Someone was blasting rap music and it was deafening. It turned my stomach a little. It was the kind with all the inappropriate language, a lot of "Nigger" this and "Motherfucker" that.

I detested it. I wasn't a big fan of the rap genre but I could give a nod toward musical differences. Obscenities and misogynistic shit just didn't go for me.

It was being played through a loud-speaker that Lorenzo had brought. Lorenzo was an undefeated 10-0 pro heavyweight who had started coming around about a month ago after moving up from the Bronx. He had some money behind him, and the manager had contacted Smitty. He tried to play the music his first time here, and Smitty had quietly walked over, turned off the speaker, and said, "We don't listen to that here."

Smitty then turned on his old-school boom box that played a combination of old R&B, some upbeat jazz and even Rock 'n' Roll. My tenure in the gym allowed for some Elvis to be played and, though Smitty wasn't a fan, it fell into the acceptable.

I had made a point of turning down the leadership job of the gym and therefore didn't really feel it was my place to address Lorenzo. I hated the message, and I hated the lyrics and, though I had some rank via my years here, I didn't really have authority.

Pig was whacking the bag today. Forty-something and way overweight with greasy hair and a face filled with acne tracks, Pig had been in the gym as long as I had. When the bell sounded the end of the round, he came over to me as I wrapped my hands.

"We gotta listen to this shit, Duff?" He looked over at Lorenzo who was stretching after a round of skipping rope. "I hate this shit."

"I dunno, Pig, maybe we're just old. Night Train, Coltrane, Grand Funk, Little Richard, the Temps and Elvis don't resonate with these guys," I said.

"I ain't puttin' up with it," Pig said. He turned and walked to the speaker. "Hey, I'm turning this shit down. It ain't allowed."

Lorenzo walked over and pushed Pig into the wall.

"Don't be fuckin' with my music, you hear me, Motherfucker. Who the fuck are you?" He got in Pig's face. Pig was tough but he knew his limits and he'd get killed if he tried something.

I stepped between the two.

"Easy, easy…" I said, and lightly put a hand on both of their chests.

"Don't fucking touch me!" Lorenzo swiped my hand off his chest with aggression. "Washed up motherfucker!"

I looked hard at him. The gym froze and with the music off it was silent. The round bell sounded but no one got back to work.

"You want some?" Lorenzo said and opened his arms in an invitation.

I put my hands up and just backed off to my corner of the gym.

"I thought so, Bitch," Lorenzo shouted and turned his speaker up even louder than it had been.

I put my earphones on to drown out the sound, which they didn't entirely do.

I felt a little sick to my stomach. I wanted to leave and never come back but something inside of me wouldn't allow that.

Chapter Thirteen

The next day Kyrone came in at two o'clock and this time he brought his fiancée Latanya. She was also a client at the clinic but in a different group. Latanya was beautiful, with light brown skin, an aquiline nose and bright brown eyes. She looked like she could be Whitney Houston's sister. She and Ky had been together since high school and Ky proposed to her when they both started on the road to sobriety.

Rocco gave them a nod, his usual greeting for customers who had been there more than once but who hadn't reached semi-regular status. I found it curious and it made me think of the somewhat odd dynamic going on in my bar.

"Hey, folks," I said by way of greeting.

"Hey, Duff," Latanya said. She was the same age as Kyrone, and I gathered they were from the same neighborhood and had similar situations that brought them to the clinic. That is, plainly speaking, probation. I think they both had minor drug charges and treatment was part of a legal diversion.

"Hey La, good to see you. Kyrone," I nodded. "Coffee?"

They nodded.

"La, how do you take it?"

"Black's good."

She had her hair pulled back in a bun, which highlighted her facial features.

"What's goin' on?" I said by way of conversation. Rocco

had the paper and would nurse his afternoon scotch for a while.

"Duff, uh, Kyrone mentioned somethin' about it bein' okay if we come in here and, you know...talk." Latanya sipped her coffee somewhat tenuously.

"Yeah, why not?"

"That Claudia took over your group and she's fucked up," Kyrone said. "She angry as hell."

I smiled a little, but it was a joyless smile.

"You okay if we talk to you?" Latanya said.

"Of course, it's okay. But you guys should know it ain't treatment and I can't write to your probation officers about anything."

They looked at each other.

"What makes somethin' treatment?" Kyrone said. "I mean, talkin' is talkin', right?"

I gave that some thought and didn't have an honest response. I shrugged instead.

"Probation's cool. He said if our urine comes back clean, we good. We been in treatment for six months, so we good." Kyrone said.

"Well, then, it's your business."

They both nodded at each other like something had just been solved. I wasn't exactly sure what, but if they were happy all it was costing me was coffee.

"Duff, let me ask you somethin'. That pain clinic that gave me the oxy and the other shit, are they supposed to just do that?" Kyrone said.

"Do what?".

"You know, 'scribin' without any real, you know, doctorin'."

This was similar to the discussion we'd had yesterday. Ky's desire to put his addiction's responsibility on someone other than himself was antithetical to recovery.

Pretty heady stuff for a bartender to ponder.

"They're supposed to be providing medical treatment. If you went in and told them you were in pain and you were convincing, a doctor might prescribe you stuff. They're supposed to be more thorough, but some are really busy."

"I just told him I heard I could get some there and he wrote me a script. Then he asked for one-hundred dollars and took my Medicaid card." Kyrone said. "That's how I got the other shit."

"You gave him your card and he asked you for a hundred dollars? Then you got the script? No, that's not cool," I said. "What do you mean 'the other shit?'"

"That special shit that was around before Uzi came out. M-Sixteen they called it. They keep messin' with the shit to create different highs. Keeps addicts comin' back," Ky said.

"The doctor is selling this shit? He isn't just writing scripts?" I hadn't heard of this. "That's really fucked up."

"See Kyrone, I told you. He a criminal," Latanya said.

"It ain't unusual for doctors to be crooked. They're just like everyone else. There are good ones and bad ones. You know if he was doing that with other people on his case-load?" I asked.

"Where you think everyone in your group came from, Duff? Shiiit, all twelve of us went to the pain clinic. Everyone on The Hill know him and what he do." The Hill referred to the ghetto neighborhood where most of our clients came from.

"He even had some boys dealin.'"

"What do you mean?" I asked.

"He give out some volume and brothers start sellin' that shit." Kyrone said.

"The M-Sixteen?"

"Hell yeah," Ky said.

"What about Uzi?" I thought of Kurth and his assignment.

"That shit came out since I cleaned up," Ky said.

"The Green Street Gangstars control that?" I asked.

"No, that's what's fucked up. I ain't with them no more but it ain't them. And they pissed."

"It can't all be coming from doctors," I said.

"I don't know about that," Ky said.

"He crooked as hell," Latanya said.

I put my hands up to slow them down a bit. This was a lot to process.

"Hold on, you're sayin' that the doctor is setting up a dealing thing through guys in the clinic? You know that, or are you just guessing? Let's not get carried away," I said.

"C'mon Duff, you can add two and two," Kyrone said.

I kept quiet for a minute and let it sink in. It wasn't my business, and though it was thoroughly screwed up, it wasn't my problem.

"If it's true, you're right, it's screwed up and illegal," I said.

"Word." Kyrone gave me his affirmation.

"Can we do anything?" La said.

"La, you trippin'. They ain't gonna believe no addicts." Kyrone pursed his lips and shook his head.

"Motherfucker fucked up my life," La said. The language didn't fit her angelic face.

They were getting wound up and I wanted to bring them down a little.

"La, let me ask you something," I said. "He take the drugs for you?" I waited. "He take the drugs for you after you got arrested for being high? Was he the one who came looking for you, or did you go looking for him."

They were quiet.

"Duff's right. We gotta keep it simple. It still on us," Kyrone said.

It got quiet for a long moment.

"I get that, but it still ain't right what he doin'," La said.

I listened. The conversation had me curious. I knew there were doctors who made money by being an easy touch for controlled substances. I knew addicts would find a way to pay whatever was asked and I knew it had been going on forever and would continue.

Ultimately, an addict just has to stop, regardless of what the rest of the world is doing.

It was a simple process. Stop. That's it.

Except simple doesn't mean easy.

Chapter Fourteen

The rest of the night was a replay of most nights at AJ's. When you had to be there and couldn't come and go as you wanted, the place lost a lot of its appeal. What the hell was I thinking, saying yes to this place?

Sleep wasn't easy to come by in my new digs with all the change swirling about. The next morning, I got up early to head to Schenectady. Billy was on standby in case I didn't get back in time to open up. I wanted to trace AJ's candy route.

The invoice I'd gotten from Harry at the lake had "Blammo" written on it. The company was still around, though I have to admit, it wasn't my favorite type of candy. They made those caramel things with the weird white stuff in the middle, they made a knockoff of Raisinets, and they made a bunch of different types of mints with red and green stripes. They also made those puffy, sugary things that sort of dissolved in your mouth after ninety seconds.

On the way north, I listened to *Elvis is Back*. It was filled with some of my favorite cuts from the period right after his discharge from the army. His vocals were wonderfully nuanced during "The Girl of My Best Friend" and "Such a Night."

It helped me pass the hour, and when I got Schenectady, I did my best to guess AJ's route. Two decades had passed so I was sure things had changed. I stayed away from places that I knew weren't that old and focused on more vintage-type establishments. I went to the Central Market on Union Street. It looked like a grocery store and the candy isle didn't tell me anything. I looked around for someone who could have possibly worked there twenty years ago. Unless they were able to work in utero there wasn't a single person who met that description. Blammo still had candies on the shelves and it looked like the same shit that they always sold.

Nothing to learn there.

Next, I went to a corner store-type grocery. It seemed like it had weathered a century or more at that spot. When I went in, I noticed that even though it was still called Nott Grocery, the guy behind the counter was Indian or Pakistani or something. I'm not xenophobic but I guessed he hadn't been there that long. Still, I gave it a shot.

"Excuse me," I said, as politely as I could. "May I ask a question?"

He looked at me and raised his eyebrows, which meant I could.

"Do you still stock candies from Blammo?"

"Yes, there," he said, pointing to the wall. He went back to his paper, which was not printed in English.

"Oh, I'm not looking to buy anything. I was curious whether you knew a man who worked for them. His name was AJ."

He gave it some thought.

"Yes, but long time ago. Nice man," he said with a slight smile.

I felt some excitement stir.

"What can you tell me about him?" I asked.

"He delivered candy. He was a decent man. He stopped working there, if I remember, quite suddenly. They brought a new guy in. He lasted a few months and then they brought another. Now, we have yet another, but I don't even know his name because they come and go."

"I hate to be a nuisance, but could you look for a name or a number I could call?" I asked.

He frowned but opened a drawer and looked through some invoices. He stopped and looked at one closer. Then he scribbled the number on a Post-it note.

"Guy's name is Kyle. That's all I can tell you."

I thanked him and left.

As I got back to the car my excitement started to fade. This didn't exactly tell me anything. I knew the current salesman of Blammo candies in the Schenectady area was named Kyle. Two minutes on the Internet might have given me the same information.

I drove through Schenectady some more but somewhat half-heartedly. I pointed the Caddie south in the direction of home. It was already ten o'clock and I really needed to be around to open the bar. I saw a pharmacy up ahead. It had a newer facade and it was a national chain, but it didn't look like it had been built within the last few years, but rather just cleaned up a bit.

I headed in and while passing through the front door I noticed one of those certificates of occupancy or whatever it's called. The place had been licensed under the name MacDonald's Drugstore in 1988. The chain probably had kept the DBA to save some sort of licensing fee or tax advantage. Again, I felt a twinge of excitement.

I went back to talk to the pharmacist, figuring the kid on the phone at the front counter would live up to my expectations of his age group.

The pharmacist had a tag that read, "I'm Scott, how can I help?"

"Excuse me," I said.

"Yes," Scott said. He wasn't quite as pleasant as his name tag might have suggested.

"Have you worked here a long time?" I asked.

He made a face. Kind of something between a wince and a scowl.

"How can I help you?" he said with annoyance.

"I'm sorry. I'm trying to find a guy who worked for Blammo

Candy about twenty years ago. his name was—"

He didn't let me finish.

"Twenty years ago? If you want to know about that, you have to call the home office, though I doubt they'll tell you anything." he put his head down and started counting.

"What do you mean by *that*?" I asked.

"Look, I've got work to do. I wasn't here back then, and I don't know about it. I need to get back to work, okay?" He went back to the shelves and started moving things around without really doing anything.

Something was weird. I realized I'd brought up something he didn't want to get into.

He kept his head down and it was clear our conversation was over. His reaction told me something had happened. It didn't tell me what. It was clear he wasn't going to tell me anything more, and I felt awkward just standing there.

I wondered what "that" was.

I needed to find out.

I headed home, and on the road back I started to think about things and try to sort things out. AJ had worked for a candy distributor, seemed to be well liked and then abruptly quit. He drifted an hour and a half south and opened up a bar. I guess that's not really earth shattering in that maybe he just got sick of the candy business. Maybe it was boring as hell and he wanted something different. Maybe he got sick of being married and was afraid of being tied down by a new baby. Maybe AJ hadn't been all that great a guy and just decided to check out.

And, most importantly, something had happened at the pharmacy. Something a long time ago and something the home office didn't want people talking about.

Did it have something to do with AJ?

My mind went back to the note. That note seemed to suggest a certain desperation. AJ had to have been involved in something dangerous. Something that even after his death he didn't want to spell out.

What kind of shit does that to a guy?
I didn't understand why it had to be a riddle.

Chapter Fifteen

By seven the boys got to the bar.

"Joan O'Salk was the Irish lady that invented the measles. That's why we get shingles now," Rocco said. He had a bit more Dewars in him than usual and he was in his authoritative voice.

"Shingles is the chicken pox, not measles," Jerry Number Two said, and nonchalantly sipped his Cosmopolitan.

"I had the chicken pox and I had zits all over me. I was only three," Jerry Number One said.

"Those weren't zits. Zits are for teenagers. You had poxers. That's what you get when you have chicken pox," Rocco said. He left the measles/shingles argument behind him.

"We had cream of tuna in the Army. I hated that shit," Jerry Number One said.

"What the hell does that have to do with anything? TC said.

"That called it that," Jerry Number One said.

"That?" TC said, his annoyance made his pitch go up.

"Shitty shingles," Jerry Number One said.

"That's 'Shit on a Shingle,'" Rocco, the military expert corrected.

"On the other hand, chicken in a box is pretty good. At least it is if the Colonel made it," Jerry Number Two said.

"Colonel Who?"

"Salk," Kelley said. He was one stool away as he always was. It was maybe the first time he had ever entered one of the

Foursome's discussions. Everyone got quiet and looked at him.

"Jonas Salk. Fucking Jonas Salk. He, not she, invented the vaccination for fucking polio. Jesus Christ." Kelley said.

"See, I told you," Rocco said and triumphantly gulped the remainder of his scotch.

I got him a new one and a Bud Light for Kelley.

"This ones on the house," I said to Kelley.

The Foursome quieted down and exchanged tidbits on the Yankees and the Red Sox and the perpetual challenge of getting a good middle-relief staff.

It gave me an opportunity to talk to Kelley.

"Hey, let me ask you something," I said.

"Oh boy. I know that tone." Kelley sipped his beer.

"I was looking into AJ's old job before he opened this place and—"

Kelley groaned. He didn't have to say anything. I knew how he felt about my detective work.

"Uh, and I found a couple of places he used to deal candy to."

Kelley frowned at me, but he was listening.

"I didn't find out anything startling. Some remembered him, some didn't. The one thing that was weird was when I asked a pharmacist about him, he got very squirrely. He said he didn't talk about that. That he wasn't allowed to, and I could call the main office, but they probably wouldn't talk about it."

"Talk about what?" Kelley said.

"Well, that's what I mean. Why would he get all weird about a question about the history of a drug store?"

Kelley looked away. He looked like he was thinking. He took a long sip on his beer.

"Well, shit, you'll find out anyway..." he said.

"What?" I looked him straight in the eye.

"About seventeen years ago a drug store owner disappeared after a shift at work." Kelley got dead serious. "They've never found him."

"What!"

"Yeah, it also made that TV show, *Unsolved Mysteries.*"

"You mean this was like, well known?" I said, feeling just a little stupid.

"Maybe the operative word was 'was.'" Kelley said. He wasn't exactly engaging, but he was a bit more forthcoming than usual.

"Why was the pharmacist so uptight if it is so well known?"

"Think about it, Genius. Would you want your business remembered for your head guy's disappearance? I mean, pharmacies are supposed to be boring, upstanding, reliable and all that shit. Having a guy disappear without a trace doesn't really help out that marketing angle now, does it?" Kelley Grouchoed his eyebrows and took a swig.

"What do they think happened to the guy?" This was getting interesting.

"Look, I'm not Robert Fucking Stack but the theories were that the guy had an affair and disappeared with the woman. That doesn't really hold up because people have affairs all the time. There's also a theory that he embezzled a bunch of money and split, but that's flawed because he was the owner of the place and that means he would have been embezzling from himself." Kelley made a face suggesting he thought the idea was nonsense.

"And what else..." I asked.

"Well, the obvious..."

"Huh?"

"Hello, earth to the Duffmeister! It was a fucking pharmacy! Duh, maybe, you know, it had something to do with drugs!" He said the last part like Jethro on the Beverley Hillbillies to emphasize how stupid I was.

"Like, he was dealing?'

"Nice, Genius. Like, uh, maybe he was doing something with controlled substances, and he had to, uh, go away because of some shit," he said. He emptied his beer and got him another without wasting any motion.

"Some shit? Like junkies were mad at him? Like he wanted

to stop what he was doing but couldn't? Like someone made him disappear for not playing ball?"

Kelley splayed his hands, meaning all of the above.

I felt like I had accomplished something. Then, I gave it a bit more thought.

"Hold it...what does this have to do with AJ's candy route?" I asked, totally confused.

Kelley laughed out loud.

"Who said it did, Asshole? You asked me about the guy in the pharmacy and why people might get weird when they're asked questions about it."

"Oh, yeah." I stopped. "I guess you're right."

"Duh..." Kelley said.

"Except it was on AJ's route..." I just let it trail off.

"Great, go ahead, Sherlock. Go right ahead."

I backed off and let it get quiet between me and Kelley. We'd covered what we were going to cover, and I tried to make some sense of it. I was confused and felt like I'd uncovered something, but what I had uncovered was pretty much common knowledge and old news. I needed some mental floss for all the overtime my head was putting in.

The Foursome came back into focus.

"And that's why to this very day Joan O' Salk is revered in Dublin for her work with the measles." Rocco said.

That pretty much summed up the night.

Chapter Sixteen

It was a long night and I closed up at two a.m. Squal came by for a beer after his shift at The Taco. It was kind of nice after a day in a saloon to talk to another in the profession.

I gave him a Narragansett and held my palms up to let him know it was on the house. It was kind of a game because bar people were insane tippers so a free beer wasn't all that "free" because I'd get a bigger tip. I held on to the tradition that the owner of a bar doesn't accept tips, only his employees, but Squal would find a way. Or, eventually, he would buy my drinks someplace else. Just another unwritten rule.

"Your new Buddy came in tonight, Duff," he said, after we had exchanged pleasantries.

That got my attention.

"Oh yeah, what was on his mind?" I asked.

"I don't think he's a real deep dude. He made a couple of comments about the pussy on the stage and how he'd like to bang the redhead and that kind of bullshit. You know, caveman shit."

For a big guy who relied on his brawn quite a bit for his livelihood, Squal was pretty evolved.

"He mention anything about me or burning down my place?"

"He doesn't talk about his 'business.' He likes to tell you that every chance he gets so he can be perceived as Paulie Walnuts. Then, he proceeds to tell you about his business." Squal paused.

"He said he took care of 'some motherfucker' who cracked wise with him.'"

"And I'm that motherfucker..."

"I'm assuming."

Squal finished the Narragansett in about two sips. I opened another.

"It's not the fifth. Did he mention anything about what he's doing in town?" I asked.

Squal burped after his last sip.

"Excuse me. Yeah, he said he had an account with someone being a nosey-motherfucker and he had to straighten that out."

"Apparently, my affection for my mom has been misconstrued. He must have someone keeping an eye on me."

"You've been nosing around? I know that wouldn't be the first time you let your olfactory organ drift," he said and smiled out of the corner of his mouth.

"I'll take ear-nose-and-throat for a thousand, Alex." I said.

He lifted his can in a mock toast.

"I went and checked on AJ's old route when he was a candy rep for Blammo," I said.

"Great name. You know it is an acronym for the brothers who owned it? Barney, Lawrence, Andrew, Mickey, Morris and Oscar Rubenstein."

"I'll take candy companies for a thousand, Alex."

He toasted me again. "What did you find out?" Squal pounded the second Narragansett and I got him a third. He'd been in the bar for six minutes.

"Not sure. Some remembered him. The Gen Yers at Central Market wouldn't get off their iPhones long enough to make eye contact with me, so I found out nothing there. The Pakistani guy vaguely remembered him and let me know that a series of guys have been in the job in the last twenty years, and then I went to the drug store and found out something interesting.'

"In Schenectady?"

"Yeah," I said. I was kind of surprised that Squal asked.

"The one where the guy disappeared way back?"

"Yeah, how did you know that?" The guy's hard drive was amazing.

"I'm an *Unsolved Mysteries* freak." He sipped the beer. He was slowing down a little. "I didn't think it made the show. I thought they didn't produce it."

I decided to pour myself a bourbon. I raised the bottle to Squal and he nodded.

"Well, like I said, I'm kind of an *Unsolved Mysteries* freak, you know, into the Internet bulletin boards and whatnot. The official story was that they didn't produce the segment, that it just didn't make the cut. The conspiracy dudes on the boards think otherwise."

He threw down the entire rocks glass of bourbon. I poured him another and sipped mine.

"What do they think?" I asked.

"They are convinced that the segment was made. That it was in the can and then someone didn't like the idea of it airing and it went away." Squal let out another burp. "Excuse me, Duff. Had the andouille sausage at The Taco."

"Who shut it down?" This was getting curious.

"Shit, Duff, who knows? They say anyone from Sam Giancana, to Sinatra, to the Men-in-Black to Antifa. I tell you, these guys get out there."

"What do you think?"

He gave it some thought.

"You know, if a T-V show was going to draw attention to something criminal I could see people involved using influence to shut it down. Who has the power and influence to do that? Who has the history of being involved in entertainment?"

"Don't look at me," I said.

"I'd guess the Mob or the government. Take your pick."

"For real? In Schenectady?"

"Tied into the Chicago family," Squal said.

"The Mafia for a thousand, Alex." He toasted me and I slid

another Narragansett in front to him.

"My cop friend, Jack Daniels, said the same thing. That's two really good sources."

Squal looked like he was mulling something over.

"I can't see the government shutting down an episode of *Unsolved Mysteries*." I poured him another bourbon. "Maybe they were getting close to solving something and didn't want it out there," I said.

"I suppose. The Mafia feels like a better fit."

"And Renzo comes from Chicago and goes to Schenectady and would come check on AJ."

"And did it every month for, what, seventeen years?"

"Yeah."

"And AJ didn't talk about it. The guys didn't talk about it and the asshole drank for free." Squal's sips were getting slightly smaller.

"Yeah."

"Sounds like Renzo wanted it clear that he was keeping tabs on AJ. That the tabs were being kept regularly and AJ was supposed to keep quiet..."

"Yeah...and I didn't tell you this. AJ left me a note to...uh...look into things that he couldn't tell me about..."

"A note? Like he knew he was going to die?"

"Or, I guess, knew like the rest of us know."

"But all of a sudden the apartment upstairs was furnished and ready for you..."

Squal did some more thinking. "What kind of thing would a guy not even get specific about even after he was dead?" It seemed like Squal was saying it as much to himself than as to me.

We were both quiet.

Squal put the glass down hard.

"You would only do that if the people you left behind were in danger," Squal said and looked straight at me.

I didn't say anything.

"Duff, be careful."

Chapter Seventeen

There was no way I was going to sleep after my visit from Squal. I had too much stuff running around my head. You have your home torched and all your possessions destroyed, lose your job and a couple of your best friends, get thrust into a business you don't really know or care much about, and it all can be discombobulating.

When I got up to the apartment, Al and Agnes started to whine. I realized they hadn't been out for a walk and they really needed one. The three a.m. double dog walk will certainly deliver you to loneliness if you're not there already. My mind drifted toward TJ and I felt something in my stomach. I had no idea where she was, what she was doing or what she was thinking. She had an ex-husband who for the longest time she thought was dead, only to find out he was very much alive. She'd lived through some really weird circumstances, and she had her own struggles with what she'd experienced in combat. She was unique, real, and like no one else I'd ever known.

She was also unavailable.

I had a habit of hooking up with unavailable women.

Usually, they aren't physically unavailable like TJ; they are just merely emotionally unavailable. A lot of them have turned out to be crazy, but the more I live the more I find a good portion of the population is crazy. Maybe it's just that people who seek to live passionately have a higher rate of craziness. Maybe they're just crazy.

I don't know why I seem to gravitate toward unavailable women. Maybe there's something in human nature that makes us want what we can't have. I never quite understood where the balance was between the needs of someone you love and your own needs. Maybe I was trying to save a damsel in distress. Maybe my whole life I've envisioned myself as a rescuer. You do that and you seem to find or maybe even create people who need saving.

I wondered about what went on inside other people. Do they get up in the morning and not immediately start worrying about stuff? Do they kiss their partner good-bye and head out for a life full of joy about what awaits them? Are they at least neutral about life and what's going on in theirs? Or was everybody living in quiet desperation all the time?

I was.

I don't always see the point in much of life. I guess what I've fashioned is a life where I seek out stuff that makes me feel intensely. It's why I love boxing. It is intense and it feels vital and important. I suppose boxing is neither vital nor important, but at least it feels intense.

I like helping people—especially vulnerable people. I like trying to see that they can turn things around. The problem is, I've learned from my years in human services that many vulnerable people are vulnerable because of stupid and irresponsible choices. Maybe it is harder for some people to make good choices, but ultimately some people just keep doing the same shit and getting the same results. Is there any point in lending them a hand if they're just going to do it all again?

Actually, I think there is. I think helping the vulnerable is what we're supposed to do.

Al came to a dead stop and commenced with focused sniffing. Agnes was forced to slow down but she went in a different direction, forcing my arms to spread out wide like I was on a cross, symbolic of my own martyrdom, or at least my desire to feel like a victim.

Al was less into the road work and more into the sniff work. Agnes, on the other hand, wanted to expend some energy. It made it torturous and annoying, rather than the slow, languishing, melancholic walk I had hoped for. It was a fitting end to a series of frustrating days.

Up ahead I spotted another dog walker. You don't get much company after three a.m. It was a woman, and she was walking a pug. Al immediately introduced himself by sticking his nose in her privates. Agnes had no interest and continued to sniff at the air.

"Sorry about that," I said. You kinda had to say that when your dog went right for the woman parts.

"Oh, no problem. Zelda can take it," she said. "You don't have an extra bag, do you?"

I didn't. I kinda felt if it was late at night and if you were on a quiet street, you could let God take care of it.

"Zelda's beautiful," I said. She was, in that pug way.

"She's from Nashville. Got her in a rescue down there."

I leaned over and gave her a pat. Then my two dogs headed into the night.

A soft rain started and I kind of liked the way it felt. I always prefer dark and rainy days, maybe because I don't feel the pressure to be happy or to be doing something outside. I'm not sure what that says about me, but I guess I was comfortable with melancholy, or at least familiar with it. Happiness, hope and optimism weren't to be trusted. They were liars and con artists.

We meandered back to the apartment, and the dogs got up the stairs a bit more easily. I filled their dishes, poured myself a bourbon I didn't need and absentmindedly checked my email. A message from an address I knew caught my eye and made my heart race.

It was from TJ

I miss you and I love you and right now I can't say anymore. TJ

That's what the email said.

That's all it said.

I felt something behind my eyes. I also felt something in my gut. There was a part of me that was relieved, but I also have to admit that another part of me was pissed off.

What the hell is going on?

Whenever TJ was back on active duty in the Army, she sometimes had to do things that she couldn't talk about. And then there were the times when she had to do things because of what was going on with her emotionally, and she couldn't talk about those, either.

Not being able to talk about things pissed me off. I think that's what people who are in a relationship are supposed to do, and when one party doesn't talk, all it does is jam up the other party. I know acceptance is the key to life and the key to happiness. Well, maybe not happiness, but maybe not miserableness, either. I don't know what the hell acceptance is the key to, but all of this was tough to accept.

Agnes, TJ's dog, the dog I got back from the Army for her, let out a long whine. I know dogs are in tune with what's going on with their people emotionally, and it was hard to believe this was just a coincidence. Al joined in with his own high-pitched hound expression.

I felt a tear roll down my cheek.

Over the last couple years, I've seen a few people die. Some of the deaths were awful and gruesome. I have also had relationships come and go. And then for a while, through my own fault, I took a few blows to the head from boxing and it left my sanity a little in question.

Of course, my sanity has always been in question. But the amount of trauma and losses that have been filtered through my gray matter have made understanding reality and exercising common sense a challenge. As much as I often hated the job of being a counselor, it did give me some anchor in this world. As much as getting punched in the face is something that I probably shouldn't be doing, just as soon as the neurological tests panned out, I went back to boxing. It was where I found sanity, it was where I found meaning, and the exhaustion of it comforted me.

The loss of AJ and now owning a bar, the loss of my trailer and suddenly being thrust into this weird place in my life had all been a bit much. I didn't know what to do. I didn't know what to feel and I didn't know how to keep going on.

And that's how things often were with me.

TJ seemed to offer the potential to give my life more meaning. There was something to her, something that made her different from other women. It's something that I could never quite grasp or understand, and I certainly never possessed it. I don't know whether the goal in a relationship is to possess someone, but there is something special about commitment and holding on and having another person be part of you. Maybe possession isn't the right word, but I'm not smart enough to come up with a better one.

Sleep wasn't going to be an option tonight. I poured myself more bourbon and sat on the couch. Al jumped onto the couch, clumsily walked across my body and came to rest in his favorite position, half on me and half on the arm rest. Agnes joined us, getting on the couch, spinning around three times and then doing her building collapse. She lay in her circle with her back gently touching me.

I let myself cry.

Chapter Eighteen

I was at the bar by eleven, getting ready to prepare for the day. I was sleep-deprived and a little wrung out from the email from TJ, but it was good to be at work doing something.

My iPhone lit up and it brought a smile to my face.

It was Jack.

"Miss Daniels, how the hell are you?"

"Hey Duff, I'm fine but I don't have a lot of time. You wanted to know about some character named Renzo?"

"Yes."

"There was a guy named Renzo Ruggiero. He worked in the Milano family, made guy, but not real high in the organization. Loan shark and criminal prostitution, that kind of shit."

"Okay, I said to be attentive.

"Thing is, he never really had to do any time. He did a couple of sixty-day things but nothing that kept him out of circulation for long. That tells me he's got people looking out for him. He hasn't had any trouble in years and seems to have seen the light and become a choir boy. Works in his church, volunteers his time with Little League, all that bullshit. Got a nursing degree when he was in the joint. Volunteers at a nursing home."

"Do you know what he looks like? Trying to figure out if it's the same Renzo".

"Six foot one, brown hair, greying temples, stocky, built like a tight end. Not like your average forty-year-old dad bod. Nose has some alterations to it."

"Any idea whether he's into something now that would be illegal?"

"I don't know enough about him. All the goody-goody stuff seems like bullshit. But I'm a cynical son of a bitch who did this shit way too long."

"Any idea why he'd be coming here on the fifth of every month to check on the bar?"

"It certainly doesn't make any sense if his new lifestyle is legit. Guys who are doing what he is doing are either collecting or intimidating. You know, making sure things are still going the way they want them to."

"I don't think AJ was giving him any money. Why would he want to be intimidating AJ?"

"Duff, that's out of my jurisdiction. And, by the way, it is out of your jurisdiction because, well, you have no fucking jurisdiction."

"Yeah, yeah, yeah, I get that a lot," I said.

"I'll keep my eye on things and put in a few feelers. If I hear more, I'll let you know."

"I got word he was in town yesterday and it's not the fifth. Makes me curious," I said.

"It should. It also should make you afraid." She hesitated. "Mind your own business, Duff."

"That's what everyone tells me." I said good-bye and hung up.

Not sure what this new information told me. Jack's description certainly didn't fit the guy I had met. Sure, the physical description fit, but there very likely could be more than one person named Renzo who fit that description. I let it run through my brain but came to no new conclusions.

I had, however, concluded something about my new profession: there was quite a bit of down time.

I'm guessing that if I ran a Chili's or a TGI Fridays, I'd have plenty to do, communicating with the home office, filling out inventory sheets and supervising and hiring staff. None of that was necessary at AJ's, and I could only polish glasses and wipe down the bar so much.

This morning, I brought the new Elvis book with me. *Destined to Die Young* wasn't exactly a cheery read but it offered more insight into the King's life than anything else I'd ever read about my hero. I was only a little into book, which detailed just how poor the Presleys and their family were. Elvis's grandparents were first cousins, and he had a couple of other marrying cousins in his family tree—not all that unusual for poor people in Mississippi in the late 1800s. The problem was, all this intermarrying probably caused Elvis to inherit some diseases that hadn't been diagnosed back then, especially if you were living in poverty.

Turns out Elvis probably had ADHD, glaucoma, and a series of autoimmune diseases that caused him to live in a ton of pain. He was also born with a deformity in his digestive tract that caused lifelong constipation. Sure, there are lots of jokes about that, but if you've ever known anyone with chronic constipation, it isn't funny at all. Add on narcotics abuse, which, given the pain he was in, was a pretty logical choice to make, and you've got a guy with a painful and messed-up insides. He took a lot of amphetamines, which is now the treatment for ADHD, and he took opioids for pain. He wore sunglasses because of a sensitivity to light that caused migraines.

Now all the jokes made about him seemed that much more unfair.

I set up my boom box by the cash register, and every day I listened to Elvis until enough customers came in to warrant a switch to ESPN. ESPN was the acceptable white noise that could help fill the lack of conversation among men. It also stimulated the vapid conversations that men were most comfortable with. Whether it was the Yanks's middle relief woes, the Giants's inability to mount an offense or Notre Dame's undeserved place in the rankings, there was plenty of fodder for everyone to have an opinion without coming close to an authentic human experience or emotion.

Elvis sang, "Only the Strong Survive" from 1968, originally done by blues singer Jerry Butler. It stirred in the background.

Boy, I see you sittin' out there all alone, cryin' your eyes out… Elvis sang, letting the pain catch in his phrasing.

He knew how I felt. He always did.

Twenty minutes after that and right around eleven-thirty, Rocco came in, this time with Jerry Number One. With two of them there it gave both of them some permission to day drink. The guys took it slow, slower than they did for the night shift, so it wasn't that much of a concern.

"Duff, you doing okay?" Jerry Number One said in an unusual show of empathy.

"Yeah, Jer, why do you ask?" I said, kinda taken off guard.

"Christ, Duff, with everything going on, you really had to ask?" Rocco said.

I smiled to myself but I also felt like I was welling up. When the Foursome acknowledged pain, it had to be pretty significant. It shattered my own denial about how much my life had gotten fucked up.

"Thanks fellas," I said. "Keeping it one day at a time." I still had a business to run and if I became a source of pity it wasn't going to be good for my personal economy.

"You sure?" Jerry Number One followed up.

Al appeared from the back room and then Agnes came in behind him. They both peered up at me. There was an uncomfortable silence. I turned toward the TV.

"Man, these guys are tough on the Irish," I said about the college football commentary. It wasn't incredibly insightful, but I hoped it sent the message that I wanted to change the subject without it getting any more weird.

Thankfully the door opened and in walked Kyrone and Latanya. They were followed by Carlton and Michelle. Carlton and

Michelle also were in the group from the clinic. Carlton was a soft-spoken, white gay guy in his fifties. He had worked in the restaurant business his whole life and got fired for stealing, not showing up, and other general addict-type stuff. Michele was nineteen, Black with long nails and heavy eye makeup. She got addicted to Oxy after a breach birth in which her baby was stillborn. Her past wasn't a pretty one and she'd been abused in about every way you can think of.

"Hey guys," I greeted them, smiling. "Coffees all around?"

"Can I have a ginger ale, instead?" Michelle said. I could smell her cologne. It was a little too sweet.

I nodded and came back with their drinks. I paused to see if they had anything specific to say. This was an odd dynamic. Was I to assume they were here for ad hoc group therapy, or were they here just like Roc and Jerry?

Actually, no one was just like Roc and Jerry.

"How's this working out for you?" Carlton said, nodding down the bar.

"It's ok. I don't know much about what I'm doing. I just make sure I show up," I said.

"Just show up…isn't that what you used to say about going to the clinic? Just show up. No matter how you felt, what you did or didn't do?" Michelle said.

It was a kind of mantra I'd spewed. What I'd meant was that you didn't have to feel a certain way to do something. You probably got more out of life making yourself do the right thing—even if you didn't want to, even if you felt like crap. With addicts I wanted them to show up doing positive things and just keep at it.

"Yeah, I guess," I said.

"'Cept you stopped showin' up, all of a sudden," Michelle said. She looked right at me. It burned a little.

"Yeah…" I acknowledged.

"After being in that group with Claudia, you shouldn't blame him," Kyrone said. "That woman is evil. Duff had to listen to her shit all day, every day."

I gave it a second. I gave it some thought.

"Kyrone, she's right. I split without thinking of you guys. I treated it like a job and didn't think of you-all. It wasn't right. At least, I didn't go about it the right way."

"You're all right, Duff," Carlton said.

I nodded. I appreciated the sentiment, and it meant a lot to me that they were here instead of at the clinic. I noticed none of them had hardly touched their coffee.

There was kind of an awkward pause.

"Duffy, what am I supposed to do with my pain. I mean, I got real pain from the C-section. Advil ain't cuttin' it," Michelle said.

I gave it some thought. She was right, of course. One of the over simplistic things that the public—shit, the addiction professionals—don't get is that addicts have real pain. They also have real mental health issues that cause pain and they have things like OCD, ADHD and everything else nod-addicts have. We like to oversimplify things and tell them to tough it out or that it is drug-seeking behavior when they ask for meds. It can be really hard to separate what is addict behavior and what is just human behavior.

"What do you guys think?" I put it to the group, just like I would've back at the clinic.

"Man, all three of us went to that clinic because of legit shit," Kyrone said.

"That's right," Latanya said.

"Yeah, that's true but..." Carlton let it hang there. He had a tendency to not want to offend anyone.

"Go ahead, Carlton," I said.

"Well, uh, just for me. I really mean, I'm just talking about myself here. I went for the sciatica pain. It was killing me. I couldn't walk, I couldn't sit, even going to the bathroom killed me," he said.

"See, I told you, Duffy," Kyrone said.

"I don't think Carlton was finished," I said.

"Sorry, Man, go ahead," Kyrone said with a nod.

"Well, yeah my pain was real, very real." He took a beat to think of his words. "But after a while, I kind of got a sense that the pain was gone, but I kept, I don't know, looking for it. I wanted to keep taking the shit. The pain was a way to legitimize it. When the doctor—my regular doctor, not the pain guy—told me he was going to wean me off, I stopped going to him. I went back to the pain guy. He upped my script," he said. He looked almost winded after that.

"Word," Kyrone said. "Same."

"Me, too," Michelle said.

"Word," Kyrone said.

I gave it a beat or two before I responded.

"Why do you think that is?"

"It's that devil in our heads, Man. That addiction voice you call it, ain't it?" That devil talks shit all fuckin' day," Kyrone said with a whole lot of energy.

"Word," Latanya said.

"How do you know when it's the devil and when it's legit pain that I gotta deal with?" Michelle said.

I looked to the four of them to find their own answer.

"I guess you listen close to what thoughts are going through your head. Then, you take the prescribed dose exactly as the doctor said. After the right number of hours, in the right amount and without washing it down with booze." Carlton said.

"And what if it don't work?" Michelle said.

They got quiet. They looked at me.

Finally, Carlton broke the silence.

"Then we live with that shit."

They stayed for about half an hour after that. The topics lightened and it became more like a group of friends having coffee, albeit at a bar, albeit that they might not be a group that would organically form in public. They had something in common which is what brings all of us together. They had each other, at least they did for today.

No one ran out to get high, no one committed a crime, and no one had a breakdown while they were here, in this moment, which is about all any of us can ever ask for. Rocco and Jerry had somehow got the remote and had switched the TV to *Law and Order*. It was a Lenny Briscoe and Mike episode. They wouldn't watch it if it was from the last two seasons. They'd go as far as the Italian guy with the white hair who was in every gangster movie ever, but after that, they'd stop. They even grumbled then about the later plots but they'd still watch.

It was the episode where the military guy's wife was bringing drugs into the country because she could sneak it in easy and without suspicion. The Navy didn't want McCord trying it and the old guy boss had laid down the law. I loved the old guy D.A. He had his shit together, didn't take any bullshit from anyone and even though he was always keeping an eye out for the political ramifications, when it came down to it, he did what was right.

There's a lot to be said for that.

McCord was grilling the Navy husband when I heard my front door open. I turned and when my eyes adjusted to sunlight, I recognized who it was.

It was Renzo and he had a friend with him. A large African American dude with a shaved head, a diamond stud in his ear and a neck tattoo of a cobra.

Subtle.

I wondered if there was an online clothier called "Badasses are Us" or "Thugwear."

He wore a leather blazer and a black T-shirt with narrow jeans. Renzo had on a suede suitcoat and a silk shirt with one too many buttons undone and the requisite gold chains.

I lifted the waitress section of the bar and walked around to meet them straight on.

"You're not welcome here." I looked at Renzo and then at the Black guy. I could feel it in my gut.

"We're not here for drinks, Asshole," Renzo said.

"Good, get the fuck out. Both of you." Renzo looked at the Black guy, who put on his best disinterested thug look.

"Just a message. I hope a clear one," he said, pausing for effect, like it was a *Sopranos* episode. "Mind your business."

Al appeared from the back room. Agnes was a few steps behind. I could hear her whine a bit. Al growled.

Renzo looked at Al and laughed.

"Hey Curtis, what if shorty gets mad, you think you could draw down on him?" Renzo said.

Curtis half chuckled. It was almost a cough.

"Get the fuck out of here," I said and took a step toward Renzo. Curtis stepped in front of him. He didn't put his hands on me, but he blocked my path.

Renzo laughed.

"C'mon C. Not now, not yet."

Renzo looked back at me.

"You've been warned." He made his hand gesture with thumb and forefinger and shot at Al.

Al didn't care for that and went into a barking frenzy punctuated with growls.

Both of them jerked, if just for a second, and then they resumed their badass posture.

"Don't underestimate Al," I said. I didn't break eye contact.

"You've been warned," Renzo said.

"Yeah, I heard you," I said. "Now get the fuck out. You hear that?"

The rush of anger and adrenaline didn't subside for a while. I also noticed the bar got really uncomfortable. Rocco and Jerry mumbled something about having to go and they'd see me later and the folks from the clinic left. All except Kyrone.

"Duffy, what the hell is going on?" he asked. "Those were some dangerous men," he added with certainty. I believed he knew what he was talking about.

"They had something going on with the guy who owned this place before me. Used to come in and check on him once a month for twenty years," I said.

"Why they do that?"

"Not sure. There weren't any payments that anyone knew about. Didn't seem to be any obvious intimidation. The guy just came in."

Kyrone gave that some thought. I could see him turning it around in his head.

"So, they just checking up on something?" he asked.

"I guess," I said. I started washing the glasses that were left behind.

"Or, maybe just reminding somebody 'bout somethin'."

I thought about that. Kyrone had a Ph.D. in street smarts. "What do you mean?"

"Well, dude just shows up once a month and sits there. Don't get no envelope, don't brace the guy against the wall, don't get a bag of nothin', don't disappear with a ho for twenty minutes...what else is there? He just lettin' it be known that he, or whoever he frontin' for, is still around. Still around or interested."

I picked up the coffee mugs and Michelle's glass as I gave it some thought.

"For seventeen years? Somebody checks in on somebody for seventeen years?"

Kyrone shrugged.

"I thought bad guys eliminated problems by whacking someone," I said.

"Yo, Duff, this ain't the movies. In real life bad guys just can't go 'round killin' everyone that's a problem. Murder and breakin' bones cause problems. Doesn't matter how bad you think you is, when you get a body, you got some trouble. People start paying attention."

That made sense to me.

"Plus, killin' ain't all that easy. Witnesses, and the idiots you get to do the killin', always wind up talkin'. It ain't like *The Godfather*, where there's some sort of honor system."

"So, you're saying this asshole came around to remind AJ of something?"

"What else? Sounds to me like he wanted AJ to know whatever it was, wasn't going away. That it's still an issue."

"That's a lot of effort to do for seventeen years."

"Word," Kyrone said.

"What kind of thing needs to be looked after and reminded about for twenty years?" I asked.

Kyrone smiled.

"What?" I said, just a little annoyed at his coyness.

"Hey, Duff? What kind of thing don't have no statute of limitations?" He just looked me in the eye, pushed back his stool and got up to leave.

"Hey, Duff?" he said, turning around before heading out.

"Yeah?"

"You be careful. I didn't say bad guys never kill. They just choose it when they have to."

I didn't say anything back.

He headed to the door but stopped again and looked at me.

"We need you, Duff. Please be careful."

Chapter Nineteen

I let Kyrone's ideas sink in.

So, Renzo had come by monthly to remind AJ of what, exactly? And what was such a big deal that they had to keep it up for more than years? Kyrone suggested something that involved no statute of limitations or something that continued to go on.

AJ didn't strike me as a murderer. The guy sold candy for crissakes.

The squirrelyness of the pharmacist resonated with me. So, a guy disappeared seventeen years ago, law enforcement hasn't found him, and they are privy to all of the available information…and they know what they're doing. I was, of course, out of my league, but just the same, I felt obliged. All I had was that AJ had sold them candy. It didn't seem like enough.

I didn't have what the cops had, and I didn't have their resources. I didn't have shit.

I decided to visit The Caretaker.

The Caretaker, whose given name was Dush Pantamanjam, was a street guy who oversaw a lot of things in Crawford. He wasn't exactly a mobster who controlled things, and he wasn't a pimp or a drug dealer. No, rather he was a sort of ghetto concierge. He knew how to get you what you wanted. Sometimes it cost you money, sometimes it cost you time, sometimes information and sometimes it cost you knowing you owed The Caretaker. All of them came with a price.

I went to his storefront on Jefferson Hill, the heart of Crawford's ghetto. It was the type of street place that sold knockoff Air Jordans, loud leather jackets, cheap pimp suits and flat-brimmed baseball hats in all different colors—usually different from the sports teams' actual brands.

There was always a twenty-something Black guy from the neighborhood working, or more accurately, hanging out, behind the counter. I was one of the few, if any, Caucasians who ever dropped by. So even though I dropped by infrequently, I got the impression I was remembered. The guy behind the counter had on a bright red hoodie with the hood up and "Say Their Names" in block letters on the front. He was working hard at looking as indifferent to me as possible.

"Hey, what's up?" I asked. There was something about being white in an all-Black area that made me conscious of how I spoke, how I stood and the words I chose. I didn't want to act Black but I didn't want to be super white, either. It refreshed my awareness of what it must be like to be a Black man in a white culture. Were all us white folks really that nasally that we deserved to be called honkies?

He gazed at me, expending the absolute minimum of energy. I might have detected a nod.

"Is The Caretaker in?" I asked, looking him in the eye and standing up as straight as possible.

"Who are you?" It came out like it was one word.

"Well, let's say I'm an old friend. Dush and I have done business in the past. Maybe I should say we had a few transactions." I wasn't starting to feel like I was in a Spenser novel.

"Dush?" He arched his eyebrows and as he said it, his mouth went crooked.

"The Caretaker. Tell him it's Duffy."

He turned and went through the curtain behind the counter with all the nonchalance he could muster.

After about five minutes he came back through the curtain and motioned me with his head to go on through. I wondered how little a guy like this had to eat to expend this low level of energy. I guessed a twice-a-week pop tart would've done it.

I went through the curtain and there he was. Today in a bespoke vested suit all in black with a black tie. His albino skin was a contrast that boldly jumped out at you. His legs were crossed like an affected movie star on a talk show. His oak desk with the banker's lamp was orderly with a leather-framed blotter and a fountain pen in its marble holder.

"Duffy, my friend, please sit." He motioned to the burgundy guest chair on the other side of the desk.

"How are you, Dush?"

As I sat, I noticed a framed five-by-seven photo on his desk. It was Latanya, Kyrone's girl.

"Is that Latanya?" I realized that I had just broken La's confidentiality because she was a patient at the clinic. Actually, maybe not. I wasn't in the field anymore and she was a bar customer. Well, sort of.

Life was filled with vagaries.

He smiled a bit uncomfortably.

"My niece. She's beautiful, isn't she? I love her." It was a rare moment of true emotional expression, maybe the first time I'd ever witnessed it.

It's a small world, I thought.

"What can I do for you?" he asked, like he was manning the lobby at the Four Seasons.

"Information," I said.

"That's something that seems to keep bringing you back. You are aware of the Crawford Public Library system."

I smiled. "Some things aren't covered by the Dewey Decimal System," I said.

He nodded and smiled to himself. I wondered if anything he ever did wasn't contrived.

"You know my policy." He paused for effect. "Quid pro quo."

"Of course," I said. "This isn't my first Caretaker rodeo."

He smiled at that.

"You know much about Schenectady?" I asked.

"Ahh, the Electric City. A town that likes its vice. I do some business there, though I am careful to stay within boundaries."

"How so?"

"Well, ah, businessmen in Chicago lay claim to many of the activities I often engage in."

"Yeah, so I hear. The drugstore thing, where the pharmacist disappeared, you know anything about that?" I asked.

He looked down and took a few beats. It wasn't that he was racking his brain to remember something. He looked more like he was deciding whether to disclose something.

"Duffy, the men in Chicago are formidable. They are efficient and smart. they don't make mistakes. They know how this game of ours is to be played. They may be seen as ruthless, but in this game, there isn't a choice to contact authorities or look to the legal system to settle...uh...challenges. So, they have become efficient." He nodded at the end of the paragraph like he was pleased at how obtuse he'd been.

"Uh, so let me see if I can still translate Caretaker-ese. The Chicago mob had some investment in a drug store in Schenectady. This pharmacist was a problem that wouldn't go away by any of the usual, uh, techniques, so they made him disappear. How's that?"

"Quite accurate," he said, and pursed his lips. He opened a drawer, pulled out a pipe, filled it with tobacco from an ornamental jar on his desk that was shaped like a Hindu god, and began to tamp down the stuff in the bowl. Then he began the process of lighting it. It was a perfect prop. I guessed he actually hated the taste, but the ritual was a priceless affectation for his arsenal.

"Um, please don't take this as disrespect," I noticed I had begun to talk like a character in a Bond film. This shit was contagious. "But I think I had that part figured out. The why Schenectady is more important. Why did they feel they had to make the guy disappear?"

"He was a pharmacist. Duffy, what do pharmacists do?" He liked doing the Socrates shit.

"They dispense drugs," I said, with just a hint of impatience.

"Yes, and what else?"

"Uh, they run a store...they inventory, they run the vacuum cleaner, they stock shelves."

He smiled.

"What would the men in Chicago be interested in?" He looked me in the eye.

"Drugs and money," I said.

The Caretaker shot me with his thumb and forefinger.

"Drugs and money..." I said. "What about drugs and money?"

He just nodded. He didn't say anything else. After a long, pregnant pause he made a grand showing of looking at his watch.

"Ahh, Duffy, my friend, I do believe I have to take my leave. There are appointments..." He paused for effect. "One thing, I know the gentlemen from Green Street are not friends of the Chicago contingent. They feel their market has been encroached."

"How does that play out?" I asked. I realized he wanted to leave but I needed a bit more from him.

"Frankly Duffy, it hasn't quite played out. You know, despite their adolescent moniker the G-S-Gs have become quite sophisticated. They are more than just local hoodlums. They have become sophisticated. They are in a quandary over what to do."

Again, he paused and sighed. "Now, I really must take my leave."

"Oh, Dush, excuse me. Thank you for your time. Please feel free to take your leave." I said, knowing he picked up on the sarcasm.

"Gilbert will see you out." He smiled. "Oh, and Duff, quid pro quo."

"Of course," I said, wondering what that would eventually mean. The dude up front held the curtain for me as I left.

"Thanks, Gilbert," I said and didn't look back.

Chapter Twenty

I did go to the Crawford library.

I went to the info desk and asked for some help. I told the librarian what I wanted to do, and she seemed thrilled to be asked about something other than where the bathroom was. She took me to the microfiche room, pointed at the boxes of Schenectady Gazettes and showed me how the machine worked.

"How do I find the right, uh, fiche?" I said.

"You have to know the date." Her name tag said Debra Wellspeak. She had red hair and was dressed in a cream-colored blouse and a long black skirt with modest pumps.

"Uh, all I know was that it was seventeen or so years ago," I said.

Ms. Wellspeak frowned.

"Then I'd get comfortable," she said, and gave me a librarian-type smile. There was something about her. The red hair, the flowing skirt, the glasses—she had that smoldering librarian thing or at least it seemed to me that she did.

"Is there any way I can find out what the date of what I'm looking for?" I asked. Actually, pleaded would've been more accurate.

"Well, what was the event you're interested in?" Debra said. I wasn't sure but I think she might've had a tiny glint in her eye for me.

"I guess some pharmacist vanished about seventeen years ago

from the Mack Drugstore that's now the Walgreens on State Street."

She suppressed a laugh and sort of rolled her eyes.

"What's so funny?" I asked.

"That's about the most famous crime in this city's history. Hang on..." She turned and headed out of the room and up the stairs. She had a great stride that turned into a trot when she hit the stairs.

She was back in five minutes with a guy who looked like hd'd answered a casting call for public librarians.

"This is Carl. Carl has been a librarian here for thirty-six years and he is a bit of an expert on this topic," Debra motioned toward him. He was an old guy, probably in his seventies, with a big neck waddle, furry white eyebrows, a crazy unkempt mop of white hair and deep wrinkles throughout his face. His Harris Tweed jacket looked like he had slept in it for a month.

"September second, two thousand and three," he said. It was like he was making a proclamation of some sort.

I wasn't sure how to address Carl.

"Carl, what can you tell me about it?" I asked.

He sort of hrumphed.

"Well, what would you like to know?"

"I'm not even sure what I'd like to know. Just tell me—" He didn't let me finish.

"Brian Barnes was the lead Pharmacist and part owner of the establishment. He generally worked from eight in the morning until ten at night. He had very few other interests and lived with his wife on Rugby Road. He had a son with autism. He worked and was a member of the Rotary. His wife died a month before his disappearance. On the day in question, he went into work as usual and simply didn't return after work. There was no sign of any struggle or anything. He just didn't come home."

"That's it, he vanished?"

"It would seem so," Carl said.

"Any theories?"

He shrugged.

"What do you think?" I asked.

He beamed. It was like in his whole life no one had ever asked him his opinion—just where to find things.

"I think he got in over his head on something with the wrong people and they had him disappear."

"Disappear or get murdered?" I sounded pretty melodramatic.

"I believe he was murdered, though whoever did it was meticulous."

"Is there any chance he just went away?" I asked.

"There's always a chance." He paused and it almost seemed like it was for effect. "But Mister Duffy, people seldom just disappear unless they have a reason. It seemed like Mister Cavanaugh had no reason to go away, especially with the situation with his son."

"So..." I was looking for his conclusion.

"It would seem to me he did not go away under his own volition but was made to go away," he said.

"Which means..." I was getting tired of him drawing it out.

"I believe he was murdered," he said, quite pleased with himself.

"By whom and why?" It was the logical next question.

"That would be entirely speculation." He sort of sniffed and changed the weight distribution of his feet.

"And what do you speculate?"

"The obvious thing would be drugs and something to do with them."

It seemed like I kept coming back to the same place. The pharmacist disappeared, probably because he got in over his head with the Chicago mob.

Too many probabilities.

There are times when I look into things and it's like pulling the thread on a worn coat. It starts out small but in very little time you have a ball of thread and a ruined suit. I think I was in that territory now.

I was down a rabbit hole, diving into the life of this poor pharmacist who was probably murdered because of something to do with controlled substances. The connection to AJ, if there was one, was that AJ handled the drugstore's candy account during that period. Could AJ have walked in on something? Could he have been involved with some sort of illicit drug thing related to pharmaceuticals? Could he have been mobbed up at the time and something went bad?

I had no answers, no sources to ask and nothing else to do. When that happened, my strategy was to just do something.

I took a ride through Schenectady. I went to the Walgreens and walked around. There was a young Black woman at the register when I walked in and she gave me a "Welcome to Walgreens." I went across the store toward the photo area, past the electronics and down the aisle by the refrigerated food.

I wondered to myself who would come to Walgreens and buy a frozen dinner or package of processed meat.

After the refrigerators, I was in front of the supplements. I couldn't help but glance at the testosterone boosters that promised me that "she'd like it, too." I took a left and went up the next aisle.

Pepto Bismol, laxatives, anti-diarrhea meds and Preparation H, all neatly arranged. Maybe they should call this the ass-crack aisle. I glanced over at the pharmacy and my nervous friend from the other day wasn't there. The pharmacist on duty looked to be an Asian woman who couldn't have been more than thirty.

I had an idea. I approached her.

"Excuse me," I said.

"How can I help you?" She sort of smiled but not with any joy. There was probably a class in pharmacy school about retail behavior.

"I have sinus congestion and the only thing that ever seems to work is Sudafed. The problem is it makes me really nervous. Is there any other alternative?"

It was a real question.

Sudafed could make me nuts with anxiety. It was like I had the choice between being able to breathe and worrying that the world was going to end or being able to breathe only out of my mouth and having my only my usual level of paranoia.

"Well, you can try antihistamines. They act in a different way and may cause drowsiness though the newer generation of them have less of a sedating effect. Have you tried Zyrtec or Claritin?" She seemed genuinely pleased to be asked for her expertise.

"I have and it doesn't move the congestion needle. Would the longer-acting Sudafed cause less anxiety?" Again, it was a legit question.

"Maybe. Would you like to try them?"

"Sure," I said. She went to the shelf and looked at her inventory.

"Generic okay?" she asked.

"Sure, same drug, right?"

"Yes, exactly. I've never understood why everyone doesn't choose generic," she said. She keyed up the computerized signature thing and asked me for my I.D. so if I was making meth out of my twelve-pack of nose pills, they could track me down. While she was absentmindedly going through the motions, I tried my plan.

"It must be kind of creepy working in the same pharmacy where that guy was murdered. But I guess when you go from being legit to dealing you kind of have to expect that sort of stuff," I tried to be as nonchalant as possible, and speak like I knew what I was talking about.

"Long before my time..." she said, still looking at the computer.

"They ever find his body or the guys who did it?"

"No, they never found anything or anyone responsible. They briefed us at orientation and said some people might ask and to not say anything. People...like you...read the papers and they're curious."

"What drugs was he dealing?" It was a little too direct, but I was running out of time.

"I guess all of the investigations came up with nothing. It didn't seem like dealing drugs was the case at all." She puttered on the cash register.

"Five ninety-nine, cash or card?"

"Card." I handed over my debit card. "Geez, you would've thought it would've been about drugs," I said, looking for a response.

"Yeah." She handed over my tiny bag with my little box of nose pills. "Have a nice day."

I walked toward the exit more confused than ever. If a pharmacist disappears in a mobbed-up town and he's a family man, but drugs aren't involved—what the hell happened?

I went through the automatic doors, turned left to get to my car, and that was when I got hit with something hard, dense and swung with intensity.

That's all I remember.

Chapter Twenty-One

"Wake up!" I felt a sharp pain in my ribs. "Get up, you can't nod here!"

I had a throbbing on the left side of my head and when I reached up, I felt a damp spot in my hair. When I looked at my hand it was covered with blood.

"I said get the fuck up!" My eyes tried to focus. There were two uniform patrolmen hovering over me. A tall skinny white guy with red hair and prominent cheekbones and a shorter, squattier, weightlifting-type Black guy.

I was a little slow on the uptake.

I got kicked again. "Hey, easy, that hurt!" I got to my feet.

"You got I-D?" the Black cop said.

I reached for my pocket, but my wallet wasn't there. My phone was gone, too. I noticed my jeans were covered in mud, and there were some bloodstains.

"My wallet's gone," I said.

"Hands up."

"Excuse me?" I asked. My brain wasn't firing on all cylinders.

"Hands up!"

I did as I was told.

The Black guy started to pat me down. Actually, it was more likely getting whacked down. He was hitting me pretty hard in what I imagined were severely bruised ribs.

"Ow! Geez..." I said. I didn't get much sympathy.

He reached into my pocket and pulled out a Ziploc baggie. The kind that would fit a sandwich.

He tossed it to his partner.

"Looks like Oxy and Fentanyl," the white guy said.

"What? That's not mine. Where'd that come from?"

"Where's the gun?" the white guy asked.

I just looked at him. "The gun?" Even as I said it, I knew it was futile.

"You match the description of the guy who held up the Walgreens yesterday afternoon, Asshole. You're under arrest for armed robbery and possession of a controlled substance."

They cuffed my hands behind my back and walked me out of the cemetery. As we went past the gates there was a sign informing all visitors that there was no loitering. A trio of street-looking people scattered when we got fifty feet from them.

"Not real bright, heading to Vail after holding up a drug store and getting high," the white cop said.

"Vail?" I said, not getting the reference.

"The cemetery. Do you even know the name of the place you hang out in?" the Black cop said.

I didn't know what universe I was in and my new friends weren't all that hospitable, so I decided to keep my mouth shut for the rest of this adventure.

They took me to the jail. It was on the bottom of Hamilton Hill in the worst section of the city. It was crowded, noisy, and it smelled of urine and disinfectant.

"You get to make a phone call. You'll go in front of the judge in the morning," the jail guard said to me without looking up from the desk.

I called Kelley's cell phone. I was banking on his knowing someone over here who could straighten this out.

"You're where?" he asked. "What the hell..."

"Yeah, tell me about it," I said.

"What happened?"

I told him what I knew.

"Geez, Duff, this is a classic. Hang tight. I know some guys there." He hung up.

They put me in a cell with a dozen other guys. Most were Black or Latin and all looked like street addicts or dealers. My head really hurt, and it felt gross, having the blood caked on. The cell was noisy with hard-to-follow conversations, some in Spanish, and others with all the street terminology interspersed.

"Duff, what the hell are you doing here?" It was Jackson. He had been on my caseload at the clinic. "Man, Duff, you was usin' all this time? Man, that shit ain't right."

"Jackson, what's up. No, I wasn't using. I was set up," I said.

He burst out in a crazy laugh, displaying his rotted and brown addict teeth.

"Oh shit, Duff, look around. We all been set up!" He kept up with the crazy laughter.

I wanted to punch him.

The hours inched by. My head hurt and my ribs reminded I'd been kicked every time I inhaled. I remembered that every client I ever had told me he was set up whenever he got busted. Of course, I called bullshit on it every time.

Yet, here I was. In jail and set up.

It was around ten o'clock when the guard from the desk came by and called my name.

"Good to have friends," he said, with the requisite guard sarcasm. "Good to have federal friends even more."

I didn't ask. I was just happy to get away from Jackson and his maniacal laughter, which hadn't relented over the last five hours. I also got to watch two different guys urinate and did my best not let it creep over to my shoes. A very large Black man with tattered clothes and ashy skin objected to their behavior and punched each of them in the head. They went down, probably unconscious. There was no intervention from the guards.

Kelley was waiting for me in the lobby. His new FBI friend Kurth was with him. They were hanging with two other guys who wore the same-style polyester suit as Kelley. I pegged them for detectives.

"Here are your buddies," the guard said as he walked me over to Kelley.

The conversation circle stopped. Kelley looked me up and down and didn't say anything.

"Thanks, fellas. I owe you," he said. They nodded and we headed out.

Kelley just looked at me. Kurth mostly looked straight ahead.

"We'll talk on the ride," Kelley said. I felt a little like a kid who got picked up at school for being in trouble and was about to get a lecture and some discipline from his dad.

I got into Kelley's Accord. Kurth drove away in his own Jeep Cherokee.

"Sorry about the dirt," I said. Kelley kept his car immaculate.

He didn't say anything. We drove in silence for about five minutes.

We came to a red light on the corner of State and New Karner. Kelley kept looking ahead.

"Go ahead." That was all he said to me.

"Um, I went to the Walgreens to see what I could find out about that pharmacist's disappearance. The guy at the library told me his theory and—"

Kelley didn't let me finish.

"Stop." He exhaled hard. "You see, that's the fuckin' problem right there. What the fuck are you doing! This shit has to stop. It's been going on for years. When you got involved with Shondeneish ten years ago it was bullshit. Then Billy, then the puppy mill, then the sex scandal at the high school..." he let it trail off.

I kept my mouth shut. He was right, of course.

"Along the way you've been hit in the head so many times your thinking is fucked up. Your judgment is fuckin' nuts."

I didn't like that. I was sensitive about comments about my mental functioning since the concussions. Coming from Kelley, it was especially hurtful. Still, I kept my mouth shut.

"What is it, anyway?" he asked.

"What do you mean?"

He exhaled.

"I mean what is this shit about? Is it wanting to be Robin Hood? Some sort of Superhero? Some crusader for justice? The great righter of wrongs? Shit is going on every minute of every day. Negative shit. It is life and you're not going to fix it. Is it ego?"

I got the sense Kelley had been holding back for years and now he was letting me have it.

I tried to remain calm. I didn't like being scolded by my best friend. I gave it some thought.

"I don't like it when the strong prey on the weak." I didn't look at Kelley. I kept my gaze straight out the windshield.

"You can't fix the world," he said.

I let that sink in. It wasn't the first time I'd heard it.

"No, I can't," I said.

The car stayed quiet until we hit the next red light.

"But it doesn't mean I have to stop fighting."

Kelley let out a sigh. "Jesus..."

Chapter Twenty-Two

The next day Kyrone, Latanya, Carlton and Michelle came in at five past two. I find it kind of ironic that they were late for this "group," just like they'd been back at the clinic. Addicts are addicts and I guess personal responsibility would always be a struggle. I set them up with coffee and got Michelle her ginger ale.

"What happened?" Kyrone said, nodding at the discoloration of my hair on the side of my head where I'd been hit. It wasn't bleeding but there was a crusty scab that had begun to form. It was tender and beginning to itch, so that it made it hard not to touch.

"I got mugged in Schenectady," I said. I figured keeping it simple, basically honest and short would be the way to go.

"I got mugged in Schenectady once," Carlton said. He said it like it was a normal thing, like "I went to the bakery once in Schenectady."

"You okay?" Latanya added. She kind of winced when she looked at the side of my head.

"Yeah, I'm fine." I tried to balance the nonchalance without false bravado. "I get hit in the head a lot." They knew I boxed.

That seemed to quiet them a little.

"Better not go to the pain clinic. He put you on Oxy," Kyrone said. The group gave that a sarcastic laugh. "Then you wind up on this side of the bar."

"No, no oxy for me." I smiled to the group.

"Yeah, that's what I said. Then the pain got so bad I couldn't think straight," Latanya said.

"Better not to ever get on it but when you're in pain it is very hard to not take something that will take it away," Carlton said.

"So, what do you do, Duff?" Kyrone said.

"You mean when you're in pain?" I gave it some thought. "I don't know. I've had pain but I don't know what other people's pain is like. I tore a rotator cuff once, I've been knocked out and I've broken a finger. They hurt when they happened but then the pain turned into a dull thing. I could handle it. That doesn't mean I know what other people's pain is like."

"The pain I had from the baby was a sharp pain that didn't go away. It was bad enough that it made me cry. The doctor said I should take something. If they knew it was going to get me hooked, why'd they do it?" Michelle said.

"Uh, I guess the theory is you take the pills while the pain is sharp and then you stop or get weaned off when it gets less and your body starts to heal," I said.

"Yeah, man, but then the pain and Jonesing from Oxy don't allow that. The pain from my back subsided a bit but my ability to deal with any pain went away, and then I got like crazy with anxiety. Who the fuck invented the shit and why?" Ky asked.

"Opium grows on a plant, morphine was derived from that, heroin was supposed to be an improvement, and everything else is a refinement of the similar stuff. The chemists can tweak it and make it do different things," I said, giving a *Reader's Digest* version of the history of pain killers.

"If they so good at tweaking it why didn't they tweak the shit out of Oxy?" Kyrone said. He was getting pissed off.

"Originally they made the intense painkillers for cancer patients. The pain from terminal cancer can be brutal and they wanted people not to suffer. This part is kind of morbid, but cancer patients who are going to die can load up on pills because, well, they don't have to worry about addiction and getting off the shit..."

Carlton cut in. "Because they'll be dead."

"Ain't that some shit," Kyrone said.

"So why did they start giving it to people who weren't dying," Michelle said.

I let that hang there for a moment because what I was about to say would be tough to hear if you went through what these folks went through.

"They changed their business model. They trained the sales force to convince doctors that Oxy and other drugs like it could be used for chronic pain in people who weren't dying. They marketed it as being safe," I said.

"That's some fucked-up shit. Did they know it was addicting as fuck?" Kyrone said.

"That's the million-dollar, actually, billion-dollar, question. They say it isn't that addictive. That addicts, well, just get addicted because, uh, they're addicts," I said.

"So, we could've not gotten addicted if we were stronger?" Carlton said. He had an angry tone.

"That's what the pharmaceutical people said. After investigations, it has been shown that they knew it was crazy addicting and covered it up. They made billions and only had to pay back millions because of their wrongdoing," I said.

"So, in plain language it was worth it for them?" Latanya said.

"Just good business," Carlton added.

I didn't say anything. There wasn't really any more to say.

Chapter Twenty-Three

Later, I got Billy to cover the bar so I could get some gym time. Billy got to the bar a half-hour ahead of time and it dawned on me what a responsible man he'd become. He had been a lost, bullied teenager when I met him who relied on a goofy karate persona he had created for himself. He had no dad, a mom who was an overwhelmed mess, and nothing to structure his life.

We got some problems solved and I turned him on to boxing and MMA stuff at the gym. He let go of all the cartoon karate stuff and learned how to fight—really learned how to fight. The one-hundred-thirty-pound, scrawny kid was now a sinewy, one-hundred-eighty-five-pound fighting machine who could box, grapple and stand in and take shots with anyone in the gym. He was also getting his master's in social work and was going to help other kids whose life's journey was similar to his.

We pumped fists when he came in, then ran down some of the beers that had to be stocked and liquor that needed to be backed up. He was quiet and it was the type of quiet I noticed.

"What's up?" I asked.

"What you mean?" Billy looked away and started putting long-neck Buds in the cooler.

"Hey, what's up?" I said, with a little more force.

He stopped and took a beat to gather his thoughts. "The gym, Man. The gym."

"What about the gym?"

"It's not the same. No Smitty and hardly any you...it is becoming something...I don't know, I just don't like." He looked away.

"Lorenzo?" I asked.

"It's not just Lorenzo. It is, uh, the environment that Lorenzo has been allowed to flourish in. It's not the gym that I remember."

"That sucks," I said.

Billy looked away and then looked back at me. "Duff, I heard the Y wants you to run it."

I got a sick feeling in my gut.

"I heard something about that. I don't want to run the gym. I'm not Smitty."

Billy looked away.

I started to get angry. "Look, Billy, it ain't my responsibility. Just like this fucking place. I didn't ask for this. I don't want this. Sure, it's fun to drink here and talk nonsense with the guys, but why me? I don't want this, and I don't want the gym."

He nodded and went back to putting beers in the cooler.

Fuck, this shit wasn't fair. It was Smitty who left, not me.

"Look, I'm gonna go get some rounds in. Thanks for covering," I said.

Billy didn't look up. He just kept stocking the cooler. "No problem, Duff," he said. He didn't look at me. I was starting to resent the hell out of the guilt trip.

The Y's about ten minutes from the bar. I grabbed my bag and I headed in. Fat Eddie, the miserable gay guy who had run the towel room for fifty years was there. In twenty-five years of working out at the Y, Eddie had been something you could always count on. He'd be there, he'd hand you a towel, and he'd insult you.

There were three guys ahead of me, waiting for their towels.

I was half in a trance after my conversation with Billy and all the shit that was going on in my life. A loud voice shook me out of it.

"Give me another towel, you fat fucking faggot before I let you go down on me!" it was Lorenzo. I looked over the shoulder of the guy in between me and Lorenzo, and I could see Eddie. His hands were shaking, and he had tears in his eyes.

Lorenzo got his towels and laughed all the way down the stairs to the gym. When I got to the counter Eddie wouldn't look at me. He just slid a towel on the counter and looked away.

It broke my heart.

No one at the Y ever insulted Eddie. Everyone knew he was an old-school gay guy who came from the era when it wasn't talked about. He was part of the gym and he was respected in his own way. I never heard anyone talk to him like that. I never saw him turn away.

Before I got down the stairs to the gym a voice called my name.

"Hey, Duff!" It was Maury, the executive director of the Y. He was a sixty-year-old Italian guy who had lived in Crawford his whole life. He'd been in charge of the Y as long as I could remember. He was a tall thin guy, with a receding hairline, a long nose and an olive complexion. He came down the stairs and shook my hand.

"Duff, where you been?" he asked. He was kind of pleading.

"I don't know if you've heard but I got this bar now and..."

He didn't let me finish. "Duff, I want you to run the gym," he paused and sort of nodded at the rap music coming from the workout floor. "You've been here the longest. You run it, will ya? It comes with a stipend. We can't have this." He had desperation in his voice.

"Maury, I'm sorry. This was Smitty's, it isn't mine. I don't want it."

"C'mon Duff, I need you. The gym needs you," he was gesticulating with his hands now.

"I'm sorry..." It was all I could think of to say.

Lorenzo was blaring his music. He had a couple of fighter friends with him and four or five other guys just hanging around.

They laughed and slapped hands on cue. Lorenzo stared me down when I walked in and then laughed.

I put some headphones on and started my Elvis playlist.

"Trouble" came on.

I wasn't looking for trouble. Not in this place.

Chapter Twenty-Four

The next day, just before two, Rocco came into the bar and fifteen minutes later Jerry Number Two followed. I was a little preoccupied, thinking about the gym and everything else, and I forgot to get Jerry Number Two a drink.

"Shit, I'm sorry, Jerry," I said.

He gave me his gentle smile. "It's okay Duff. I'm guessing you've got a little on your mind these days." He raised his Cosmo.

I just nodded. It was a kind response and I appreciated it.

"You sure you want to do this?" Rocco said and gazed around the bar.

I gave it a second. I didn't want to hurt anyone's feelings. Not here, not now.

"Sure, I guess," I said. I didn't have a lot of conviction behind it.

"They going to do anything to that asshole who burned down your trailer?" Rocco asked.

"I don't think they have anything on him," I said. I wiped down the end of the bar.

"Can't they prove he bought the Johnny Walker? I mean how hard would that be?" Jerry chimed in. I looked at the clock and it was one fifty-five. The group would be in any minute.

"Kelley tells me they did check all the local liquor stores, and no one had a sale of Johnny Walker that day. Or, at least no one who wasn't a regular. Best we can tell, this guy is only here once a month."

They thought about that.

"Can't they do all that fire forensic stuff. Check the, whatchacall-it, the antagonist," Rocco said.

"Accelerant." Jerry corrected.

"I'm talking as fast I can. You in a hurry or something?" Rocco said.

"Kelley told me they didn't find any trace of accelerant. Whoever set it knew what they were doing. Probably experienced at torching places. It is a skill that comes in handy for some lines of work."

I checked my watch. It was five after. Maybe the group was taking a day off.

Al sat up from his bed in the corner and started to grumble a little.

"Uh-oh, someone just ordered lunch," Jerry said.

I threw together some turkey from the cooler and a pasta salad from the last time I'd ordered out. I handed the mixture to Jerry.

"You mind serving the prince?"

"Of course not." Jerry flipped a napkin over his arm like a Four Seasons waiter and presented the dish to Al. "Sir," he said, as he bowed and then returned to his stool.

"Wait for it..." Rocco said.

Agnes appeared in the doorway. She let out her whine. Jerry bounded off his stool.

"Yes, My Lady? Lunch?" Jerry said.

I repeated the dish routine. Two-twenty. I didn't think the group was coming.

Jerry presented the bowl to Agnes. "Ma'am..." he said.

Agnes took a second to look at what she was getting. She gazed up and down and concluded that the portions were fair and that the contents were identical to Al's. There would be no reason to try to trade up.

Two-thirty. Maybe they had had enough. Maybe the novelty

had worn off. Maybe they needed to be compliant with their official program or risk getting in trouble with probation or endangering their welfare benefits. I told myself it was okay.

Before long I felt the recurrent guilt from abandoning my job at the clinic. I told myself it was just a gig and not a moral obligation. It didn't feel right even if logically it was pretty sound.

At three-fifteen the door swung open and I was surprised to see Trina. She hadn't visited the bar since I'd taken over and we'd had far fewer interactions since she got married. Nothing spoken, always cordial, just an acknowledgement and respect of her marital status. She didn't get off until four.

"Hey, look who's here! Little early—did you finally have it with her bullshit, too?" I wanted to keep it light. We had our past and we'd both moved on. Anything we felt would remain unspoken. It felt weird but it seemed right.

Trina stood by the bar stool and didn't break a smile. She didn't move to sit down. She didn't respond to my barb.

"What's up?" I asked. Something wasn't right.

"The guys that come and see you..." she trailed off.

I got it. She as going to tell me I was in some sort of trouble.

I wasn't going for it. I didn't work for Claudia anymore and she had no power over me. I was a barkeep and that was all.

"Look..." I started to say, getting ready to make myself clear.

"Latanya overdosed." She just blurted it out. "She's dead."

With that she started to cry. She turned and ran out.

I flipped open the waitress gate and ran out after her. I got to her just as she got to the door.

"She relapsed, well, of course she did, obviously. She took that, what's it called, Uzi or something. It's supposed to be stronger or do something," she resumed crying. "I don't know much about it but there were five O-Ds in Crawford last night."

"They were in here yesterday. She seemed fine." I said it almost to myself. "Where the hell did they get it?"

Trina had pulled herself together a little.

"I think from the pain practice they went to. That's where

they always got their stuff," she said, sniffing and wiping her eyes.

"Dammit, that guy's going to pay," I said. I felt it inside me. Time for the doctor to pay.

I focused my attention back on Trina. "You okay? You want me to drive you home?"

She looked at me. "I've seen that look before, Duff. You're going to go do something stupid," she said.

She knew me better than anybody.

I kissed her on the cheek and headed back into the bar.

I yelled into the bar and told the guys to help themselves. They'd gotten used to doing that and they'd leave cash for what they took.

I was going to the pain clinic. My heart was pounding, and I could feel the cold sweat on my back. Trina was right, of course. I was about to do something stupid.

But I couldn't not. No, not now.

There were times for well-thought-out, rational strategy and there were times for action. Yeah, I often regretted the action, but I also hated, really fucking hated, laying back when I felt something needed to be done.

And something did.

Something really did.

It was time to make a visit to the pain clinic.

I went up Central Avenue and over Wolf Road, dealing with the streetlights. My heart pounded, my mind raced, and my blood was full of adrenaline. It happened to me like this, and when it did, I couldn't think. I had to do something physical. I think most of the time boxing kept it in check, kind of a preemptive exhaustion of it, but with a hiatus from the gym it wasn't titrated at all.

The clinic was in the corner of a newish strip mall. There was a retail tile shop, a chain guitar/music store and a disgusting all-you-can-eat Asian joint. I put the Cadillac in the handicap spot and headed inside. It was a half-walk, half-trot, but my heart rate was up like it was a full-fledged sprint.

The lobby was full. Some of the faces looked familiar from my clinic experience, not people from my caseload, but patients who were in an out. I couldn't recall their names but their faces and how they looked at me jogged something in my memory.

"May I help you?" the receptionist with the jet-black pixie cut and bright red lipstick asked. She was pale and vibing some sort of Goth look.

I briefly made eye contact but ignored her smug disingenuous offer to come to my assistance. I spied the layout and headed toward the door to the left of the reception area. It had no sign or window, but I was certain it opened into the clinic.

"Where are you going—you can't—" She didn't get to finish.

I ignored her and threw the door open. There was a hallway that went in both directions and I took a left. The first door said, "Examination Room," and I went in.

Nothing.

Ten feet down the hall there was another. I pushed it opened and heard a couple of startled gasps.

"Who are you, uh, uh, you can't just..."

He didn't get to finish. I looked at the thirty-something Black guy in the room. He had on ridiculously baggie jeans and a multi-colored leather jacket. His Yankees cap was red on red, and the sticker was still on the brim, which hadn't yet been shaped.

"Get out!" I said to him. He was big and he looked like he knew about the streets. He also knew that crazy people can fuck you up and should be avoided. He left the room.

"You can't come in here—" The doctor wore a white lab coat, reading glasses and was balding. He was a shade over six feet, had a gut, and looked soft.

"Shut the fuck up," I said. It was the sort of thing that came out of my mouth in moments like this.

I slapped him hard with my open right hand and he sort of whimpered and slid off of his plastic seat.

I put one knee on his chest and placed my right hand on his throat. It was a move I'd learned way back in my karate-training days, called "Tiger's Mouth." You could control a man, or kill him like this, depending on the amount of pressure you applied.

"My friend Latanya is dead. She stayed clean for a couple of months and then she came back here."

He gasped. I let up on his throat to allow him breathe.

"She told me she was in pain. I gave her what she asked for."

"You gave her something new. Something different. Something stronger. Uzi, or some shit."

"I treated her pain."

I applied more pressure to his thorax. Enough for him to realize he could die soon if I was crazy enough. I wasn't sure how crazy I was.

"The truth! Give me the fucking truth!" I shouted and pushed the pressure into his throat. He gagged, spit something up and began to choke on it. I let him feel that for a few moments. I thought of Latanya. I thought of Kyrone.

He began to convulse.

I let go and he rolled onto his side with his knees up to his chest in a fetal position and began to puke. It was pinkish, which told me he'd hemorrhaged something in his throat or esophagus. I should have felt bad.

I didn't.

He began to sob. In between sobs he puked some more.

I took his seat and watched him.

"Is the money worth it?" I said with as much righteous condemnation as I could muster.

He brought a hand to his neck and rubbed where my hand had been. His eyes remained closed and he half-wept and half-writhed. Part of it was physical but I sensed something else. Part of it was psychological.

He was breaking.

I've seen it before. I've seen guys' guts ripped out. I've witnessed a guy take a spear in the throat. I saw a head literally get blown off.

Watching a man break psychologically was worse.

"They make me. They fucking make me. They'll kill my family. They make me." His cries turned into a wail.

I just watched him. There was no talking to him like this.

I waited.

His chest heaved. his face winced and he cried some more. It started to slow. Like I said, I've seen it before and I've learned that the body has a mechanism that won't allow the psychological pain to totally destroy a man.

He cried, but it lessened. He wiped the snot from under his nose and sat with his knees up and his arms around them. He didn't look at me. He looked at the floor. He acted like he didn't care anymore that I was there.

I waited.

His breathing slowed. He struggled to stand up.

"You have to leave. This is a doctor's office." He did his best to compose himself. He went to open the door. I put my hand on it and pushed it closed.

"Talk to me," I said, glaring into his eyes.

He looked away.

"I don't even know who you are. I certainly am not going to—"

"I think we've established that I'm a little fucking crazy. So, we can go back to the other way, if you want."

It was a hollow threat. Something had changed. Something had made this not so simple anymore.

He exhaled long and hard.

He looked at the floor.

"I've been threatened. They have threatened my family, my wife, my three-year-old and my new baby. They check on me. This isn't my business—this isn't my practice. I do what they tell me because of what they'll do if I don't," he said. It was forced. He didn't want to talk, but I could tell that there was some relief.

"Who?" I asked.

It was the million-dollar question.

"I'm not even sure. There's a guy who comes around. There's stuff I have to send in the mail..."

I cut him off.

"Chicago?"

He just stared at me.

"How'd you know?"

"How'd they get to you," I asked.

"Look, I don't know who you are or what brought you here, but I don't feel like telling you anything," he said.

"I might be the only hope you have," I said.

"Yeah, how's that?" He was back to himself. Back to the rational doctor who has learned to deal with the nefarious stuff he had gotten himself into.

"I'm not a cop. I'm not with the health department. I'm a guy who cares about the addicts who are dying. I care enough to try to do something about it."

He just looked at me. He shook his head and sat down. Sort of collapsed down in his chair.

"I was working for a hospital and decided to go into my own practice. I wanted to help people who dealt with chronic pain. Not just with medication but with physical therapy and with exploring surgical options, that kind of stuff."

I just listened.

"It was tough without a big hospital affiliation. Tough to get referrals, tough to get the insurance companies to put me in their plans. I was losing money. I have a wife and two kids. I'm a fucking doctor and I wasn't making a living."

"How can that be? I thought doctors were set," I said.

"Everyone does," He exhaled hard. "You have any idea what my student loans are like? Do you know how much liability insurance costs? I have to pay for all the electronic record-keeping, the staff salaries and benefits. It's a big nut and I don't have any business acumen—I'm a fucking doctor."

"I guess I never thought of all that," I said. And I hadn't. I thought even the bad doctors were rich.

"So, one day this guy comes in. Doesn't even really say who is he. He seemed to know about my financial situation. Says he's helped other private docs like me turn things around. He wasn't from a hospital or H-M-O or anything. He was just a guy."

He looked down at his shoes. I got the impression he was relieved to talk to someone about this.

"He says if I just started prescribing a specific medication, he could make it worth my while and that it was a totally legit drug that was great for pain. It seemed like a plausible plan."

"What happened?"

"You already know what happened. I started prescribing the drug and patients struggled with getting off it. Then, the same guy would show up like clockwork and check my numbers. He'd let me know I needed to do more, prescribe more and get more people in. He said he would put the word out and I started getting an overflow of patients. They were promised they'd get the opioids they wanted. Then they started having me sell other stuff. I'm not even sure what it is."

"What other stuff?" I asked.

"It's some other sort of opioid. The addicts say the high is great. I don't even know what it is. It scares the hell out of me. It has been a few things. M-Sixteen was one, now it's Uzi. I have no idea what it is."

"Is that what Latanya got?"

"Yes."

"And it was made clear that you were to keep doling it out," I paused, "or what?"

He hesitated.

"They had me up against the wall. They could turn over the evidence that I was dealing, and I'd lose my license and maybe go to jail. That was enough, but then the guy showed up at my daughter's day care. Sent me photos of my little girl with him on the playground. He was letting me know he could get to her."

"What's the guy's name?"

"I don't even know. The billing goes through some third party and they take it right off the top. I'm not even sure how they're doing it or when the health department and the attorney general will be coming knocking on my door. In the meantime I can't even tell you who these people are."

He held his face in his hands for a moment and then took a deep breath, shaking it off. "I don't know what else to do but keep doing it. I'm in so deep, and I'll never risk my kids and my wife. I just won't do it."

"People are overdosing. You get that—right?"

He just nodded.

I knew I shouldn't, but I felt bad for the guy. He'd made a greedy deal with the devil, but he was just a guy who'd made a bad decision that he now couldn't get out of.

"You don't know the guy's name that you deal with?"

"No, I send records to A-B-C Billing. Then a check comes to me from A-B-C billing, paying me. The money's good but it makes me sick to my stomach to take it. My wife doesn't know any of this. I don't know what she'd do if she knew about the photo with Maggie."

"You from Schenectady originally?" I asked.

"No, I'm from outside of Trenton, New Jersey."

"I recently learned that this is a mob town and that it's controlled by a crime family in Chicago. You're dealing with the Chicago crime family,"

"Jesus..." He looked like he was going to throw up. "The Mafia? I'm being extorted by the fucking Mafia!"

I let that just hang there for a moment. The guy was in a pathetic situation.

"You said you knew of other clinics dealing with the same situation."

"More or less. I mean no one comes out and says they're being extorted but if you listen carefully and read between the lines, you can make a guess."

"You want this to change?" I asked. I looked into his eyes. His eyes met mine and then he turned away.

"Of course, I do, but you didn't exactly sweeten this whole deal by letting me know I'm up against the Mafia," he said, rolling his eyes.

"If I could fix it so you could, though, you'd go for it?" I wasn't even sure what I was suggesting.

"Of course, but not by putting my family in any danger. I wouldn't want any part of that.

"Leave that to me," I said. I realized how grandiose and falsely heroic I sounded. It wasn't the first time in my life I'd made such a promise.

"So, you're going to change this?" he asked with quite a bit of disbelief in his voice.

"Yup," I said.

Now I just had to figure out how.

Chapter Twenty-Five

I got back to the bar and tried to slow down my thoughts, heartbeat and breathing.

The Foursome left early, and Kelley didn't come in, so the bar was mostly empty most of the night. One by one the boys had filed out and soon I was left by myself. I started to wipe things down and get ready to close up and head to the apartment. After a moment or two, I hit the Elvis slow songs playlist and poured myself a bourbon instead. I had some things to go over in my head.

Latanya was dead. She O.D.'d and it happened right after I left my job. Sure, she came in here and she probably did as much therapeutic work here as she had in the clinic, but I couldn't help but think her death had something to do with me.

Then there was the role of the doctors. Guys who I thought spent their entire formative years preparing to keep people from suffering and dying before they had to. Now I was seeing them as ruthlessly greedy, like any of the rest of us. Shit, they made good money, why did they have to reach for more.

Elvis was into the second verse of "It's Midnight," lamenting about how he gets weaker as it gets later. I knew the feeling.

And addiction. I didn't know where it fit in. Sometimes to me it seemed like nothing more than a name we gave to bad behavior. Calling it a disease—I just didn't know about that. If you had cancer through no fault of your own and had to go through chemotherapy and all that hell, wouldn't you find calling addiction a disease a bit insulting?

And pain. What was pain? Could we nail it down and say a person was in this or that degree of pain, or is it all subjective? Could it be that pain might be nothing more than a fancy word for something endured by people who don't know how to deal with life's discomforts? I mean I know some people who've lived with more pain than I can imagine, but there are plenty of other folks who've lived with bad pain all of their lives and never said anything about it or took anything more than an aspirin.

Kyrone and Latanya had legit pain, but enough to ruin their lives with something else? You had to know when shit was out of hand, didn't you? I mean I know addiction is cunning and baffling and all the shit the twelve-steppers say but, come on, people knew when it was too much, didn't they?

I sipped the Jim Beam and reflected on my own hypocrisy. I guess I knew better, somehow, and I knew I was in control. Maybe that's what every addict said. Maybe I'm a lot more fucked up than I want to believe. Where was the line? Where was the line for anything in life, and what the hell did it matter anyway? Seemed like it all ended in shit anyway.

Elvis had his reasons. Damn it, he did.

I just listened to him sing.

Did Latanya have any less legit reasons than my hero? Than I?

What was pain?

And emotional pain? Who can put a meter on that?

Lack of toughness? I couldn't make myself believe that was all of it.

I thumbed through the new book and found a chapter about Dr. Nick. He was Elvis's doctor who claimed he was the only one trying to control an out-of-control patient, that he was treating the pain. The pain.

The pain.

The pain clinic started out treating patients just like Elvis. People in pain who needed help. They got it. They needed a product and they needed it more and more. Or at least their addiction told them that.

It was bad.

And the pain clinic was bad.

It was about money.

The pain drugs were about money.

Getting rich off another's pain, or at least another's weakness, was despicable.

There was something nagging me. I had been meaning to make a phone call, but I felt foolish about it. I had put it off a few times, but I think now was the time. I checked my contact list and called the number.

"Boggs," came the flat, emotionless greeting.

I had met Boggs in Las Vegas at what used to be The International Hotel, now called The Westgate. He was a union foreman stagehand. He had worked the stage on the crew in the seventies. He met Elvis a few times. Boggs gave me the TCB medallion that Elvis gave him. That, along with every other possession I loved, had gone up in flames in the fire.

"Boggsy, It's Duffy."

"Holy shit, holy shit! How you doing, My Man? What's goin' on?" I could hear some real joy in his voice.

"Well, to be honest, probably a little too much. Quit my job, lost my girl, my house burned down, and I inherited a bar," I said, giving him the elevator speech of my recent life.

It went silent for a moment.

"You're not kidding are you..."

"I wish I were, brother."

"What can I do?" He was sincere but I knew that he knew there was really nothing either of us could do.

"Probably nothin', but I do appreciate it." I paused for a second. "Any word on Angelyne?" She was a young Mexican woman I had helped out of a bad situation a few years back with Boggsy's help.

"Steady work in the chorus of one of the Cirque shows. She

also has a Monday night lounge show here opening up for a magician. Some dude named Cory Haines. They got a good thing going."

"That's awesome. How's the brother?" Her kid brother is autistic and when he was in Mexico, he wasn't getting any services. A couple of Mexican fighters and I had helped him get into the United States.

"Last I heard, she told me he was doing great. Goes to program every day and has a supported job in the kitchen at The Orleans," he said.

"No shit!"

"Yeah, something we can both feel good about," he said. "Hey, Man, it is great to hear from you but what's up? You usually call when somethings going on?"

"Yeah, I guess you're right. I feel a little funny asking about this."

"Duff, it's me. C'mon, Man..."

"It's an Elvis thing," I said, kind of sheepishly.

"Usually is. What ya want to know?"

"I know about the drug thing. I know he had, uh, trouble. Lately, I've been seeing a lot of guys around here getting addicted to pain meds. I wanna know, I guess, I wanna know if you saw him in pain."

It felt weird asking. Like I was a curious fan. I guess I was, but it was something more important than just fan curiosity.

Boggsy took a few seconds to answer. Then he spoke.

"One night when he and the guys walked by on the way to the stage he turned and said to Esposito, 'Man, it hurts so fucking much,' and he bent over, then took a knee and cursed. Esposito said he'd cancel, and Elvis said 'fuck no.'"

"It was bad?"

"Duff, I don't know how he did it. Five minutes later, he hit the stage all smiles and did all the Elvis things like he didn't have a care in the world. It was a great show that night. When he left the stage and was out of view, he went to one knee and moaned. I felt so bad for the guy."

"How often did shit like that happen?"

"That was the worst I saw it. Another time he came over to say hi and he told me about his headaches and how he had to wear the shades that night on stage. He hated to do that because the fans wanted to see his face," Boggs said.

"Damn," I said and gave my next question some thought. "You think, I mean, you think the pills were legit?"

Boggsy didn't answer right away.

"Duff, the man was in pain, but there's no doubt he overdid it. He was so out of it some nights. Man, I watched them give him a shot of something to wake him up before he went on. I mean, I know he was in pain but I'm sure he took shit outside the recommended doses."

He had a resigned tone to him.

I didn't say anything for a long moment.

"Ever see anyone deliver that shit to him?" I really wanted to know.

"Ah, can't say for sure but I saw guys come in with bags and give them to his boys. Wouldn't be surprised if it was the shit. Weaselly looking motherfuckers, you know? Assholes."

"Yeah, I got you." I thought about things for a second. "I mean, Elvis was hurting, and doctors gave him stuff and he got addicted. Shit, Boggsy, whose fault is this shit?"

"Duff, c'mon, people a whole lot smarter than me and you don't know how to answer that question.

"Yeah, Boggsy, you're right. One of my ex-clients O-D'd today. She got addicted to pain meds. Then well, honestly, she got hooked and abused them. I can't get my head straight about it."

"You, me and the rest of the world."

We signed off a little after that.

Chapter Twenty-Six

When I woke up the next morning my mind was already spinning.

I wanted to get a better sense of what Renzo did and what he was all about. I gave some thought about following him, but he already knew me and my orange El Dorado was about a block long and very hard to disguise. None of the Foursome had the patience to follow someone without getting distracted by some shiny object along the way. Kelley was mad at me and I didn't want to ask Billy.

I gave Squal a call. He lived enough in the underground world that it didn't seem like that much of a stretch for him, so thought it might fall within his comfort zone. He also seemed to have almost as much distaste for the guy as I did.

He didn't disappoint me.

"Say the word, Duff. And we're in luck. He mentioned he'd be here today the last time I talked to him. Some more bullshit about his accounts," he responded on the phone. "Would it be okay if I kick his ass, too?"

"Uh, as much as I'd like that, it probably wouldn't serve the overall goal," I said. "At least, not yet."

"Got it. Any idea where I can pick up the tail?"

"I don't know. The airport?"

"Yeah, of course. He's always bitchin' about how fat the attendants have gotten and how he wouldn't even fuck them now.

Like they're all dying to screw him."

"A real charmer," I said.

"I'll give a full report," Squal said.

"I owe you one."

Rocco and Jerry Number One came in right after I opened. I wasn't very talkative and let ESPN fill in the gaps. Nothing made sense to me. The human condition, pain, weakness and escape. There didn't seem to be an explanation that covered all of it and every theory left something big out, at least in my mind it did.

I just didn't understand.

The day seemed to crawl by, and I began to wonder about spending my life doing this. It seemed like a life sentence for brain death. God in heaven, Man, how long until I started having the same attitude toward life that AJ had had? All day with the ESPN talking heads was brutal. I couldn't take their self-referential smugness and I couldn't take the ridiculously slutty outfits on the women. It drove me crazy with its inane-ness.

Yeah, I was beginning to realize how AJ got to be AJ

Fortunately, that night Squal dropped back in.

I cracked a Narragansett and slid it in front of him. He gave me a quick nod.

"You're not going to believe this shit, Duff." He took a sip big enough to take in half the can.

"Try me," I said.

"Our buddy spent most of the day volunteering." He lifted his eyebrows.

"Excuse me?" I wasn't sure I'd heard him right.

"Yeah, that's right, he's a fucking philanthropist." Down went the rest of the can. I replaced it and cracked it open.

"And?" I asked. Squal only drank a third of the can this time.

"He volunteers at a group home for people with developmental disabilities," Squal said. As big a guy as he was, with more street behind him than ninety-five percent of the world, he was woke enough to not use the 'R' word.

"He what?" I said.

"He left the airport. Had breakfast on Fuller Road at Inga's and then went through Guilderland to Schenectady. He went down Union and turned off on Rugby and went into a place on Partridge. I sat there for two hours. Then he came out with four residents and went for a ride."

Beer gone. I opened another.

They went for a ride out to the Briggs Kill preserve. Then the five of them went for a hike for about an hour and half. After that they got a pizza at DeAngelo's in Rotterdam."

I just stared at him.

"Yeah, I didn't believe it either. Then he took them back to the group home. From there he drove back to the airport and left on the seven-fifteen flight to Chicago."

"That's it? He didn't pop in here today."

"Well, he's sent his calling card already. He doesn't want to lose his edge by being redundant."

I let it get quiet for just a beat or two. Then I just had to ask.

"Squal, I just don't get it. You get a feel for anything? I mean, no hookers, no drugs, no money exchanging hands?"

"Only if you account for the two pizzas at DeAngelo's."

"If you had to guess, what would you think was up with the guy?"

Squal twirled the empty can and I realized I was behind. I cracked a new one and slid it in front of him.

"This one has me baffled. I mean what kind of scam can you be doing while you're taking a bunch of guys with disabilities for a hike?" He took a regular, human sip.

"What's the program name?" I asked.

"Resources for Living. They're a pretty big outfit. Got homes and a school and all sorts of programs."

"I knew an addictions counselor who relapsed and went to work in that field while he rehabilitated himself. I can reach out to him. Squal, I owe you."

I extended my fist for a bump and got one.

"My pleasure. I know it might be awkward with T-J and all,

but come on down to The Taco sometime. I could use some reasonably intelligent conversation most nights."

"Reasonably is the best I could do," I said.

He headed out.

I set up the Foursome with drinks. They were discussing the merits of the Richard Gere mice rumors. I let them continue while I made a call.

I hit up my old friend Ernie who worked for RFL. He picked up right away.

"Duff, what's going on? I'm a little busy." His smart phone went in and out and I imagined he was changing ears. "Doing an outing with the guys."

I loved how guys who worked in the disability field had their own shorthand. "Outing" was going out and doing something rather than staying in the house. "Guys" was the euphemism for the people with disabilities. It sure was better than the 'R' word but it still seemed, I don't know, maybe a little patronizing.

"I got a question about a guy who volunteers at the Partridge residence," I said.

"Duff, I've only subbed and done per diem there, but I'll try to help out. Whatcha want to know?"

"This guy Renzo is volunteering. What you know about him?"

"Oh shit, yeah, I know Renzo. Comes once a month all the way from Chicago. Said he fell in love with the place when he lived here twenty years ago and wants to help out. Gave money to furnish the place, for repairs and for the above-ground pool. Takes the guys for hikes."

I just couldn't reconcile that this was the guy who burned down my trailer.

"Who are the guys?"

"You know Duff, I'm not supposed to use last names." Ernie said. All of us in human services know the rules. All of us broke them.

"Yeah, I know, Ernie. I won't go anywhere with the info. I

wouldn't ask if I didn't need the help."

I heard him exhale into the phone.

"Walter Louis, Michael Kensington, Edwin Barnes and Sean Stevens," he said, maybe a little faster than normal.

"Barnes, Edwin Michaels?" I repeated.

"Yeah, that's it. Duff, we're going into the theater, gotta go."

"Ed Barnes. Ed Barnes," I repeated it to myself.

Barnes is a pretty common name. It's not Smith or Jones but there's a lot of Barneses and people with disabilities who come from all over to live in group homes. And what did it even tell me? Brian Barnes is the missing pharmacist. Renzo, who perhaps is really a darling guy, maybe just wants to even the karmic decks by doing some good works.

Why?

Why would this ex-con who has supposedly gone straight come from Chicago once a month to visit a group of adults with disabilities between threatening me, intimidating me and burning down my house?

It didn't fit.

I called Ernie back. I didn't care if he was in the theater.

He didn't pick up. A moment later I got a text.

"In the theater," it read.

"One question. Who is Ed Michaels's father?"

"That's easy. He's dead. Been dead a long time. So is his mother. RFL is all he has."

And apparently Renzo.

"Thanks." I signed off.

What the hell did that tell me?

Nothing.

Hold it, maybe, something.

It was time to pull on the string again.

Squal had told me they went for pizza and a hike. I decided to put my shoes in their footprints. Billy agreed to cover the bar for a few hours while I followed my craziness. I took a ride to see where they'd been and figure out if that would tell me anything.

I had heard of DeAngelo's. It was an old-school Italian palace in Rotterdam that was famous for its pizza. They had a bar and kind of a quirky one at that. The waiter wore different vests every day and between that look, the padded bar and the paneling, it was 1967 all over again. I went in to see what I could see.

There was the famous bartender.

His nametag read, "Cheech." His vest was a shiny burgundy today.

"What can I get you, Pally?" He had a three-pack-a-day voice.

"Carry Schlitz?" I said, without much hope.

"My favorite since I stole it out of this very cooler from my dad forty years ago."

He opened a long neck and seemed quite pleased with my order.

"A long neck—look at that!"

"Yeah, not easy to get. I got a Milwaukee connection. My buddy runs a machine shop out there on Fifth Avenue. They treat it like a micro-brew out there. Overcharge for it, but I don't care. It makes me feel like it's the sixties all over again."

"You'll have to hook me up with the guy," I said, trying not to overdo the enthusiasm.

"Jordan. Lives right by the Harley museum."

I didn't know where to go with any line of questions, so I took a chance.

"Hey, how's my friend Renzo? He comes in with the guys, doesn't he?" I tried to sound natural and I think I failed.

Cheech went cold. The smile left his face and he started wiping down the bar.

"Renzo? I don't know no Renzo," he said, and disconnected the eye contact and busied himself with bar tasks. Sometimes somebody clamming up speaks volumes.

I finished the Schlitz and Cheech didn't seem to be in a hurry to get me another. Something about bringing up Renzo hadn't sat well.

It sure hadn't.
I showed myself to the door.
The message was Cheech didn't talk about Renzo.
The why was unclear.

Chapter Twenty-Seven

I took a ride to the Briggs Nature Preserve. I didn't expect to find anything more than boring trail markers, trees, babbling brooks and chipmunks but I didn't have anything else to do. Besides, the YouTube videos on self-improvement that I've been watching keep making the point that being out in nature is good for the neuroplasticity of the mind. I made a mental note to find out what exactly neuroplasticity was.

The trail head announced this was overseen by the DEC, that there was no motorized bike use, no alcohol or drug use, that dogs must be on a leash and littering was a one-hundred-dollar fine. All good to know, even though I didn't plan on doing any of them. I got about thirty feet into the trail that headed straight in from the parking area. It was before the brush became heavy.

There was a guy there.

Just a guy, kind of heavyset, wearing dirty New Balance wide sneakers, a windbreaker and dad jeans. He wore glasses and a plain navy-blue ball cap with no insignia. He was carrying about forty more pounds than he should have, and his belt intersected his belly so that there was fat above and below it.

There was something familiar about his form or the way he moved. I couldn't place it. Then, it dawned on me that he was a former client from the clinic. Jimmy had a sex addiction in addition to alcoholism, and part of his routine was anonymous rendezvous with other men in places where you were unlikely to get caught.

Places exactly like this.

He turned away but there was really no place to go except farther into the preserve or to turn and walk right past me. It looked like he was just trying to disappear or hope and pray I wouldn't acknowledge him. I didn't break stride and just kept heading down the trail.

"What's up, Jimmy?" I made an effort to be as matter of fact as possible. The guy didn't need any more shame in his life. His last name was Clark, but I remembered that the other guys at the clinic called him "Crackass." I had no idea why and really didn't want to know.

"Hey Duff," he said without eye contact. I didn't say anything else and resisted the temptation to try to be therapeutic in the moment. Jimmy was probably drunk, which numbed the shame of doing what he did and seeing me had probably shocked him out of his anesthesia. I felt bad for the guy.

A hundred yards later I came across an abandoned ten-speed bike and some beer cans. The Bud cans were so old the elements had yellowed them, and the ten-speed was rusted, the tires split from age and being out in the air.

I wondered how this had occurred.

Had a bunch of kids with a twelve-pack ridden a bike into the woods? Did they get so drunk they couldn't ride the bike home? Had they stolen the bike and the beer and didn't want to get spotted? Shit like this gnawed at my psyche. It was unimportant and I wondered whether other people wondered about the same things.

Up ahead about another fifty yards was a pile of old magazines. They were porn magazines from the early nineties. Empty beer cans and porn magazines were always a staple in wooded areas, that is, until the Internet came along and mom-and-pop shops started to crack down on underage drinking. Kids used go into the woods to take a peek at magazines other kids stole from the store or from their Old Man's stash, and drop them out in the woods. It was a real sense of community from pre-adolescents and adolescents, and the unspoken use of pornography probably went a long way toward explaining people's strange sexual impulses.

Just ask Jimmy.

Today, kids had smart phones and unlimited access to, well, just about anything. I shuddered at the thought and wondered if I had had a smart phone as a teen if I ever would have left the house.

Yikes.

There was a footbridge over a creek and a sharp turn in the path. The path went down an embankment and into a bowl in the preserve from what used to be a reservoir a hundred years ago. It had dried up and now created this stadium-like feel to the bowl. You could stand around the ridge and look down at the brush and vegetation that had grown over what had been the reservoir floor.

Down the ridge, about a quarter mile away on the reservoir floor there was a steel shack. No path to it and it was rusted and looked uninhabited. It had no windows and from my angle I didn't see a path in or a way out. It was probably something that the DEC had built for rangers or others who had cared for the preserve in the past. I didn't have anything better to do so I walked toward it.

It wasn't an easy walk. there were switches, branches and brambles and it was rocky under foot. I thought to myself I wasn't sure what the difference was among a switch and a bramble and a branch, but in my head, it seemed that there was no need for a delineation. With fifty feet to go I saw there was a chimney on the top of the roof on the side away from me. It was more a pipe than a chimney, and as I got within twenty feet of it I saw a small curl of smoke coming from it.

This led me to believe that perhaps the place wasn't uninhabited.

As I got closer, I noticed a vinegary smell. It was pretty strong, and it was unpleasant. It had a solvent odor under the vinegar. I walked around the building and saw a door in the middle of the steel shack. This side had two windows, and both were cracked. My instincts told me to be careful, that this had a creepy and dangerous feel to it.

Many times throughout my life I had wished in hindsight that I had paid closer attention to such feelings and obeyed them. Once again, I was about to ignore them and be disobedient.

I opened the door.

It was poorly lit but as my eyes adjusted, I could see it was an elaborate chemistry lab, complete with beakers, Bunsen burners, metal racks, powders and bottled liquids. A glass bowl with a brown powder was on a table next to what seemed to be the main work area. I dipped my index finger into it and applied it gently to my tongue.

It was bitter and I spit it out.

Then a voice came from the door.

"Who the hell are you?" the man yelled.

"I guess I have the same question. Something tells me you're not with the state department of conservation," I said. I looked closely at his face. I was a good fifteen feet away, but it was him. I recognized him from the news clippings Carl had showed me.

He had a look on his face that was a combination of anger and confusion.

"This is private property and you're trespassing," he tried to sound like a badass but it was weak and he knew it.

"Something tells me that cooking heroin or whatever else you got going here doesn't really get you to claim trespassing," I said.

"Who the hell are you?" he asked again.

"I don't know, Barnes, but for a guy who disappeared a long time ago and who left a town scratching its head, I'm not sure you're in a position to be asking identity questions."

He looked around at his lab and went to move toward a cabinet. Instinctively, that seemed like something I should prevent.

"Why don't you stay where you are?" I asked. Actually, it was more of command. "What exactly are you making here and for whom?"

He ran to the cabinet, opened it and pulled out a handgun.

"Get out!" His eyes told me he was a crazed and desperate man.

I didn't move.

"Get out, I said!" His voice cracked.

"Look, you—"

He fired the gun. In the metal shack it was deafening. It didn't hit me, but it would be a long time before my hearing would be normal.

I turned and ran out the door. I ran through the brush and up the ridge, back to the trail with my heart pounding and my chest heaving. I got fifty yards away and turned to see he wasn't following.

I looked at the shack and saw there wasn't any smoke coming out of the chimney.

He must have run right after I did, but in a different direction.

Chapter Twenty-Eight

I raced back to the bar, my heart pounding with adrenaline. I wasn't comfortable with running but there is a time and a place for bravery. It may be a cliché, but guns are the great equalizer, and it made no sense to stare down the barrel of a gun and do something stupid. Barnes ran the other direction and that told me that being found out was his number-one concern. I bet he was speeding off to tell someone important that he'd been found out. I had a good guess who that someone would be.

I wanted to make sure I was there when Kelley and Kurth came in, which was usually a little after their shift. Sometimes it was a little after five and sometimes it was a little after nine.

If I hurried, I could get back by five.

There was a part of me that questioned what I had just seen. A pharmacist goes missing for nearly twenty years, and I start looking for him and he turns up within a week? That kind of put me in Lenny Briscoe status.

I got to park right out front by the entrance. Billy's pickup truck was still there.

When I went in, I saw Kurth at the bar drinking a Bud Light. He and Billy were in conversation.

"I don't know if I'd say that Crawford's drug problem is huge. I mean, we got one, there's no doubt about that, but every city and town on the Hudson up from New York is a stopping place for dealers," Billy was saying.

"Let me ask you this; you're a young guy, could you tell me where to find a dealer if I asked?" Kurth said.

"I don't know if I could tell you who was a dealer, but I could find someone who could. Sure, that wouldn't be any problem," Billy said. It didn't surprise me. Billy hung out at the boxing gym, had done a social-work internship and had been part of the social services system for years. He knew how the street worked.

"Hey Duff," Billy said.

Kurth lifted his bottle in a salute.

I thanked Billy for covering and he offered to restock the coolers and wipe things down. I told him he didn't have to do that, that he could get going.

That left me and Kurth.

"Where's Kel?" I asked.

"Dunno, he was supposed to meet me here half an hour ago."

"Kelley is almost never late," I said.

"Yeah, well there were a series of assaults at Crawford High, so he might've got mired in that bullshit."

I nodded.

"Hey, I got something. Maybe something really big…" I said.

He tilted his head and smiled. "Kelley was right about you. You stick your nose where it doesn't belong, don't you?"

I frowned at him. "Yeah, yeah, yeah…you know that asshole, Renzo, the guy who was harassing AJ and burned down my trailer?"

"Allegedly…" Kurth said, and smiled.

"Screw allegedly," I got myself a Schlitz out of the cooler. "My buddy, Squal, the big guy that comes in here once in a while…"

"The bouncer at the strip joint…"

"That's him. He followed Renzo on his last trip to town. I guess he spends his time volunteering with disabled guys. Pizza, hikes, cash—a regular do-gooder," I said and drank some beer.

"Not exactly thug-like." He finished his beer, and I slid a fresh one in front of him.

"No, but it might still be thug-like after all. I got a friend that sometimes works in the group home that Renzo visits. One of the guys has the same last name as the missing pharmacist—"

He interrupted. "What's the name?"

"Barnes."

He made a motion with his hands like it wasn't a huge deal.

"I know, not the most unique name. That's not even the wild part. I followed where they went on a hike. It's a place called Briggs Kill Preserve. Nothing special, just some nature trail, has the remnants of an old reservoir in the middle of it. I hiked it and went off the trail just a little. I found this metal shack. It had a small chimney with smoke coming out."

"Yeah so? Probably a D-E-C hut or something," He looked at me hard.

"I went in. I found Barnes. It was a laboratory. He shot at me and I ran. He ran in the opposite direction."

Kurth put his beer down, wiped his mouth with the back of his hand.

"You sure it was Barnes? I mean, they've only ever used that one photo and it has been years."

"It was him. It was a lab. He was cooking something," I said. I looked right at Kurth.

He finished the rest of his beer. "You know exactly where it is? Can you lead me there?"

"Yeah," I said.

"Let's go."

We headed to the preserve.

I drove at about ninety on the thruway. I figured I didn't have to worry about traffic offenses with a federal get-out-of-jail card on the person with me.

"Kelley's impression that you have a habit of sticking your nose into shit that isn't your business is dead-on, isn't it?" I could tell he was trying to be matter-of-fact.

"Yeah, he chews me out whenever he catches me," I admitted.

"Probably doesn't want to see you get hurt."

"Well, I'm a big boy who makes his own decisions, albeit not always good ones or sane ones."

He just nodded. We got to the Schenectady exit and I wound my way around the city, using 890 until I got to the edge of town and then I took the Hetchertown Road to the preserve.

"You might get your Florsheims dirty," I said, as we started on the trail head.

"The price the well-dressed hero pays," Kurth said. He was trying too hard to be affable.

Jimmy, the ex-client I'd spoken to earlier on the trail, was just in again from the start of the trail. This time he had a friend with him. It was a waiflike, early twenty-something guy with his straight blond hair pulled up into a man bun.

"Hey, what's up, Jimmy?" I asked. "Still here?"

"Hey, Duff," he said with some reluctance.

I didn't want to think about what transaction was about to transpire.

"You know that troll?" Kurth said. His inability to celebrate diversity didn't surprise me.

"Former client at the clinic I worked at."

"Man, I don't know how you deal with them," he said.

"After you get to know people you start to realize we all have more in common than you think. Everyone hurts, everyone gets sad, everyone is pissed off."

"I guess..."

We walked another half-mile, went over the footbridge and made the sharp turn. I walked to the edge of the ridge and waited for Kurth to catch up. He was twenty feet behind me.

"What the hell..." I said. It was almost a yell.

Kurth had caught up with me.

I looked down the ridge at the reservoir bed.

The shack was gone. There was a rectangle, faded grass and rubble in its place.

"What the hell... It's gone," I said.

"The shack that was here a few hours ago?" He had a tone

of disbelief.

We walked down to examine the footprint. There were fresh tire tracks heading out and up the utility path to the dirt access road.

There was nothing in the plot. It was just dirt.

"Somebody wanted this gone in a hurry," Kurth said. The situation had that cliched feel of a cop TV show.

"Somebody with access to labor they can get immediately," I added.

Kurth looked around. The ridge was all around us. "This is a good spot for a lab. You can see people coming from all angles." He looked around, turning slightly to take it all in. "Let's get out of here."

I could read his mind. If we had any company, we were sitting ducks.

Kurth's pace was entirely different on the way back to the trail. We didn't speak until we got to the trail head. Jimmy was still there but his companion had gone.

Kurth stopped before we headed to the parking lot.

"You think your friend saw anything?" he asked.

"Let me find out."

I walked over. Jimmy didn't walk away but he didn't look me in the eye, either. "Hey Jimmy," I said, trying to be non-threatening. A guy like him was easily threatened. "You see anything happen with the shack that was down there?"

"Will I get in trouble?" he asked. Still no eye contact.

"For hiking? Of course not." We both knew I wasn't addressing the elephant in the room.

"A bunch of guys came in a big pickup. They had tools. I think most were Mexican. They had that thing down in fifteen minutes."

"You recognize anyone? Hear any names?"

He thought for a second. "The Mexican guys were working their asses off. It was amazing."

"Anything stand out? Any names?" I asked.

The only name I heard was when they were talking to the guy in charge.

"What was that?"

"They called him, 'Senor Renzo.'"

Chapter Twenty-Nine

"That's your friend that burned your trailer, isn't it?" Kurth said.

"I didn't ever hear the title 'Senor' when he was around, but it sure as hell sounds like him." We were heading back to the El Dorado. We didn't speak again until we pulled out and were on the road.

"I know Kelley tells you to mind your business," Kurth let his voice trail off. "Ah, never mind."

I hated when people did that.

"What?" I said with a slight dash of annoyance.

"Nah, it's just that..."

Again, with the trail off.

"Kurth, I barely know you and I'm sure you didn't get to be a D-E-A agent by being mealy-mouthed. Spit it out," I said. It was more than a slight dash.

He took a second like he was gathering his thoughts.

"I know Kelley gives you shit for sticking your nose where it doesn't belong," I had no idea where this was going. "But I'm federal and we have a bit more leeway when it comes to operations."

I waited to hear more. It wasn't forthcoming.

"And..." I said.

"Well, I'll just come out with it," he said.

"About fuckin' time."

"Would you want to help us bring down Renzo, the Chicago connection, the pain clinic...the whole operation? We don't think our undercover people would be credible. We could use someone new to the drug trade."

"Hold it; this guy, Renzo, hates me and I hate him. How do I connect with him?"

"You could see the light as a former drug counselor. See that this new Uzi shit is irresistible, that the bar isn't doing so good and you could do it for one score, some shit like that. Get your buddy Squal to join you. Didn't you say Renzo likes him?"

"I don't remember saying that, but that is the case. Squal travels in more of those circles than I do. Renzo would listen to him. What are you thinking?"

"You guys look to make a buy. Say you want to start something a little south of Schenectady in Crawford. Give the gangbangers in Crawford some competition."

"How do we do that?"

"You get the word to him. Let Squal do it. You set up a buy. Have Squal get as many senior men involved as possible. When the deal goes down, we swoop in. We bust Renzo, shut down his operation and seize his product. I can't think of better revenge." He smiled out of one corner of his mouth.

"Me either." I liked the sound of all of it.

"One thing..." He winced.

"What?"

"I'm a little on my own on this. The agency allows that for some of us. But..." He winced again.

"What?"

"I can't get the money. At least I can't get it by myself. Do you or Squal have any resources on the street to back you? They'll get the money back at the bust. Right there."

"How much are you talking about?"

"The more the better. A hundred K, two-fifty would be better."

"A hundred thousand? Two-hundred-fifty thousand? What the fuck!"

"I know, I know... I shouldn't have brought it up. Bad idea.

Never mind." He shook his head and looked out the window.

I let a long moment pass while I did some thinking.

"Now wait... I might have an idea," I said. I didn't want to lose out on nailing Renzo.

"Nah, forget it, Duff."

"I can get it. I definitely can get it." I got that feeling I get when I know I'm doing something crazy.

"What the hell are you going to do?"

I didn't want to say it out loud. But I knew. I definitely knew.

It was time for another visit to The Caretaker.

Chapter Thirty

That night I was a little too on edge to go through all the Caretaker rituals. There was now too much at stake.

"Let him know I'm here," I said to Gilbert at the counter.

He looked up at me, momentarily moving his gaze from the *New York Post* sports section.

"Nobody comes in here talking like that. Disrespectin' the shop." He tried for the relaxed but intimidating look. I wasn't having it.

"Yeah, yeah, yeah...tell him I'm here," I said and returned the hard look.

He took a full minute and a half to get up and go through the curtain. He had that kind of roll and bop stride that I'm sure he'd been honing for years. He was back out in a minute.

He motioned with his head for me to go back.

"Mister Duffy, Gilbert tells me you were a bit unpolite this evening," he made a tent with his fingertips and looked up over his wire frames, which, I would bet, had no prescription in them. "That's not like you."

I ignored the comment.

"I'm sorry for your loss." I nodded at the photo of Latanya.

The smile left his face. He gave me a hard look.

"You have no idea..." he said. I think he teared up, but in an instant, he swallowed and went back to his persona. "What brings you here this time?"

"I'm going after them. I'm bringing them down. I need your help." I knew I was being intense, and I knew it wasn't how he liked things. He made a motion with his hands, palms facing me, imploring me to calm myself.

"I'm serious," I said.

"The last time we met on a related topic I let you know that these individuals are from or have their roots in Chicago. I've kept myself from involvement with them. We have led a peaceful coexistence. I'm not interested in changing that."

"Latanya was clean. She was making a go of recovery. She was trying. Kyrone was, too. This new shit they've developed is something we haven't encountered. She tried it and she died. Isn't that enough for you?"

His face lost all expression. I could tell he was thinking.

"Talk to me, Duffy. What is your plan?" There was none of his cartoon theatrics now.

"I found the pharmacist. He was cooking shit in a shack in Briggs Kill. He saw me and pulled a gun, so I ran out of there. Six hours later the shack was gun. A witness saw this character Renzo there. He was the guy intimidating AJ. He comes to town once a month and volunteers with some guys from a group home. One of them is the pharmacist's son. I'm guessing Renzo made a deal to take care of the kid as long as the pharmacist kept cooking and making new variants of the shit that killed Latanya."

"That's a hell of a story." He paused to think. "So, again, what's your plan?"

"A federal agent contacted me about setting them up for a deal and then getting them arrested with the shit. It's tight and it'll work," I said.

"But that Renzo hates you and you hate him. Why would he believe you'd want to deal with him?"

"Money for one, and my friend Squal knows him. He thinks Squal has his back."

"The bouncer at The Taco?"

"Yeah."

"He's formidable." He nodded as if to give it some thought. "What does any of this have to do with me?"

"I need a quarter-million dollars." It sounded absurd as I said it.

He just looked at me.

"You get it back right after the deal is done. The fed promised. And nothing comes back to you."

He glanced almost imperceptibly at the photo on his desk.

"That's a considerable amount of resources."

I just looked at him. I leaned over the desk and picked up the photo. I looked at it for a second and then placed it gently back down.

"Come back tomorrow morning at eleven," he said.

I called Sqaul on the way back to the bar and asked him to meet me at the bar. It was late but he was a bar person, and the time wouldn't bother him. A quarter-million-dollar drug deal set up to frame members of organized crime deserved more than a phone call. I made sure the Narraganset was iced.

Rocco was in but he was engrossed in the newspaper.

"I'm in."

It was all Squal said when I outlined the plan. He drank most of the can.

"Think it over," I said. "I know it's a lot to ask, Man. This is pretty heavy."

"How many deaths, how many ruined lives can we trace back to the asshole? Burning your place, whatever he did to AJ and his family and your client Latanya. If I can be part of something like that, I'm in. I don't have to think about it."

"We need to have a plan," I said.

The front door opened as Kyrone came in. I hadn't seen him in a few days. He sat down at the bar, halfway between us and Rocco.

I interrupted Squal to check on him.

"What's up? What are you doing here so late?" I asked. Kyrone was looking down. He sniffled and his eyes watered.

He was trying to center his breathing, but it wasn't working. He went to look at me but only glanced and went back to looking at the floor.

"I used." He put his hand over his face and cried.

I didn't know what to say. I poured him a coffee. I motioned at Squal and slid him another can. He waved knowingly back at me.

"It was that Uzi, the new shit. Like no other high I ever had, Man. I went out for three days."

"When was your last?" I asked.

"This afternoon." He shook his head. "I fucked up, Duff."

"You've been through this before. Twenty-four hours at a time, right?"

"C'mon, Duff, fuck that bullshit."

I didn't say anything for a moment. I had just hit him with a cliché and I hated myself for it.

"Look, Kyrone, stick around. I gotta finish things up with Squal over there," I said.

He just nodded. I stood in front of him for a couple of beats and reluctantly returned to Squal.

"He's hurtin', huh?" Squal asked. I positioned another beer in front of him.

"Yeah, real bad." I just shook my head. "So, I don't know where I was. This Kurth guy, the federal agent, said go ahead and set it up and his boys will come in on the deal and shut it down."

"Yeah, tell me more." He gulped from the can.

"I gotta get a quarter-million dollars." It sounded ridiculous.

Squal spit his beer, spraying me and the bar in front of him.

"Yeah," I said.

Instead of asking anything he just raised his eyebrows. I knew that meant I'd better explain.

"The Caretaker will lend us the money because he knows he's getting it back."

"That psycho? We're in bed with The Caretaker? Jesus, Duff!"

"I've done things with him before. He's kept his word."

"Jesus..." He finished the can. I replaced it. He took a deep breath.

"Okay, Okay, what's my role?"

I figured you could float it with Renzo. Tell him you want to set something up here. Get the Uzi going for Crawford. Squeeze the Green Street boys. He'll eat that shit up, won't he?"

"Definitely. If I can tell him the girls at The Taco would be into it, he'll light up like a Christmas tree. He gave me his number. I can call him. He's always asking me to buy in to his operations."

"Great. I'm getting the money tomorrow. See if you can get in touch with him. I'll clue Kurth in and we'll set up the deal. He shows up with product, we hand over the money, Kurth charges in, and we bring Renzo and his bosses down." I was getting excited.

Honestly—it was half fear and half excitement.

Chapter Thirty-One

The next morning, I fished Kurth's business card out of my jeans and called him.

"Great, set it up for tomorrow," he said. He wasn't asking he was telling.

"Tomorrow? Uh, shit, I could use a little more time. It's not like I have a lot of experience doing quarter-million-dollar drug deals."

"Duffy, don't fuck this up. I got word Renzo is coming to town today. If Pasquale can talk to him this morning, he can have the product tomorrow and it can go down. Any delay fucks this up," Kurth said. His attitude had changed from seeing me as a guy doing him a favor to someone he felt comfortable ordering around.

"All right, all right, I'm getting the money today. I can call Squal and set things up."

"Great, let me know the time and I'll take care of things on my end."

He hung up without another word. The guy wasn't exactly a ray of sunshine but if it meant putting a scumbag like Renzo away forever, I could put up with a lot.

I dropped by The Caretaker's, had my usual bright and cheery interaction with Gilbert, and got into see Dush without much trouble.

There was a large gym bag on his desk. He looked at me and

nodded at the bag. He didn't do any of the usual Bond villain shit. I guess a quarter-million bucks will suck the affectation right out of anyone.

"If the Green Street Gangstars get wind of this, there may be trouble," he said, without his usual accent.

"Why is that?" I asked.

"You're entering into their business. They don't take kindly to that."

"But I'm setting up their competition to get busted.

"They don't know all the behind-the-scenes bullshit you've set up."

It was interesting to hear him talk like a human being. I could hear the street in his voice. "You'll have the Chicago mob and the G-S-Gs wanting to kill you," he said, and looked at me.

"Making my impact both locally and nationally," I said.

"Yeah, Duff, it is real fuckin' funny." He just shook his head and sat back in his chair.

He tented his hands and exhaled hard. "You know, Latanya was the closest I've ever had to a daughter." He was talking more to himself than to me. "She was precious and at the beginning of her new life."

I didn't say anything.

"Revenge is for suckers," he said, looking at her picture. "I don't care. I want these motherfuckers to pay for what they've done."

He waited a long moment before he looked up at me. "Duffy, don't fuck this up."

I don't think he was talking about getting his money back.

Chapter Thirty-Two

Around eleven that night Squal called.

"He's in. Totally went for it. Three guys coming in from Chicago to do the deal. Barnes will be there, plus his big African American buddy, Curtis." I could tell Squal was pumped. "Wants to do the deal in the Briggs Preserve in the reservoir."

"Why there?" I asked. I didn't see the sense in it.

"Likes the idea of having everything in front of him where he can control it. Some wild, wild west bullshit, or something."

I waited a beat. "Squal, you still okay doing this?"

"Fuck yeah. How many times do you get to right a wrong and bring down a really bad guy?"

"The Caretaker says the Green Street Gangstars are going to be gunning for us after this."

"Oh well, we'll deal with that when it comes," he was feigning a little too much matter-of-factness.

"Tomorrow at five-thirty a.m. as the sun is coming up," Squal said.

"Got it. I'll let Kurth know," I said.

I called Kurth and he picked up on the first ring.

"Kurth," he said, just like on TV with that perpetual impatience.

"It is set for five-thirty tomorrow when the sun's coming up," I said.

"Yeah, I got that from my intelligence. He's bringing three

upper-level guys from Chicago. They're hoping this turns into a regular deal. They like the idea of spreading the market with Uzi."

I hesitated and then asked what was on my mind. "You got any advice?" I asked. The guy had started to annoy me.

"What do you mean—advice?"

"Look, I'm in and all that but I'm a counselor, a fighter and a bartender. I haven't done a lot of quarter-million-dollar dope deals. For that matter, I haven't screwed over a mob family, either."

"Just do what we said. You and the big guy, Squal, get there when you say you will with the money, and then take the product."

"Uh, and when do you and your men come in?"

"Duffy, like I said, as soon as the money is exchanged, we drop in, arrest them and you get to walk away," he said, like it was the easiest thing ever. "And don't tell Kelley."

"I'd have thought he could help."

"Fuck, Duffy, listen to me. This is a federal thing. We don't want the locals screwing it up. He's not briefed. He doesn't know what's going on and he doesn't have the background. This is the culmination of a two-year project."

"If it's a two-year project, how did I get involved three days ago?"

"Don't be an asshole. You presented a unique opportunity and we jumped on it."

I thought that over. "We?" I asked.

"This isn't exclusively my show. We have a task force that I communicate with constantly. We had hoped something like this would present itself. And you presented it."

"Got it," I said. It felt a whole lot less patriotic than it had when I'd first heard it.

Chapter Thirty-Three

Squal and I got there at five a.m. There were no other cars in the lot at the head of the trail. Just me and Squal.

And our quarter-million dollars.

We took the trail like I had done the last two times I'd been there and got off and walked to the bowl. The patch of grass where the cooking shack had sat reminded me of all that had gone into this. I looked around and wondered where the FBI guys would be, how they'd go undetected and what it would be like when they dropped in to foil the whole thing. Would it look like a scene from NCIS? Somehow, I doubted real life would be as cool.

"They're late," Squal said at five thirty-one.

"Geez, a bunch of criminals who have exploited vulnerable people for years and caused who-knows-how-many deaths and they don't have the courtesy to be on time," I said.

"I guess I'm just a little on edge," Squal said. He looked straight ahead. He was holding the duffle bag and hadn't laid it on the ground.

"A little? I'd be shitting my pants right now if I'd had anything to eat in the last thirty-six hours."

I heard a car engine and saw a set of headlights appear at the top of the bowl behind us. There was a slight clearing in the brush at the head of the access road in the direction Barnes had run after shooting at me.

They cut the headlights and the SUV rumbled down the uneven ground. It was an Escalade, and apparently, they didn't care what such a trip was going to do to the suspension.

The SUV came to a stop twenty feet from us and there was long moment before the doors opened.

When they did. Renzo stepped out first. Two guys who looked just a little older than he followed. Sure to stereotype, they wore velour track suits. The one guy was short and fat with a really bad jet-black toupee and deeply pitted acne skin. The other was a bit taller, a bit thinner, with a bald head and a gold cross hanging out of his warmup suit. Barnes came out last.

Curtis was driving and he came out last—leather jacket, sawed-off shotgun and black Ray-Bans, despite the fact that the sun wasn't all the way up. His black boots had a fresh shine to them, and he had to be pissed that they'd be covered in dirt by the time this was over. He must've read Spenser books because he was styled after Hawk.

Renzo walked toward us. His swagger was even more obnoxious than before.

"Squal, you gotta keep better company. How'd you get connected to this piece of shit?" Renzo said.

"Fuck you," I said. It was a reflex. It might not have been the smartest move to antagonize him.

"Renzo, his money is green," Squal said. *Snappy gangster comebacks for a thousand, Alex.*

"Let's get this shit done," I said. It was going to be great to watch Kurth and his men ruin these guys.

"Curtis!" Renzo called. No other direction.

Curtis went to the Escalade, opened up the back and came around with a W.B. Mason cardboard box that would've held copy paper. He stood next to Renzo.

The short fat guy spoke up.

"Lemme see the money," he said.

"Lemme see the Uzi," Squal said. I'm not sure how he thought of shit like this in the moment.

The fat guy pursed his lips in annoyance then nodded to Curtis. Curtis lifted the box lid off and held it toward us.

"I want to taste it," Squal said. Just like in the movies. I'll take drug deal protocol for a thousand, Alex.

The fat guy exhaled. He nodded again at Curtis.

Curtis took a knife out of his leather jacket, hit a switch and it opened up. He stabbed one of the bricks and presented it to Squal. Squal ran his index finger over it and put it on his tongue.

He looked at me and did his own nod.

"It's good," he said to me.

"All right? Can we get the money and get the hell out of here?" Renzo said. "Once this hits the street, you're gonna want more of this soon. I guess if Duffy's money is green, I'll keep taking it," he laughed.

I walked over and handed him the duffel. Curtis handed Squal the box.

And then, we waited for Kurth to put all this to an end.

They all walked back to the Escalade. They got in. Curtis started it up and they took off up the side of the hill.

And, nothing.

Chapter Thirty-Four

We looked at each other and didn't say anything while we watched to Escalade struggle halfway up the hill.

Squal spoke first. "What the fuck?"

"Yeah," I said.

"Where the hell are they?"

I didn't say anything.

Squal dropped the Uzi.

Nothing.

We waited.

Nothing.

Squal broke the silence. "You realize how much time we would get if we got caught with this shit?" Squal said.

"I'd rather not," I said. "Fuckin' Kurth!"

That was when the sky lit up, followed by a series of explosions.

There was some sort of fireworks show going off at the top of the ridge. A series of Roman candle explosions, flashing light and popping loudly with mini explosions and sparkly fire pinwheels. Strange to see a fireworks show at daybreak.

Oddly enough, the light was all green.

The show went on with one explosion after another as the lights were shot into the sky, followed by fluorescent-green explosions. It was startling to say the least, and Squal and I were transfixed as we looked into the sky.

Then the green Roman candles and the rat-a-tat of the explosions stopped as suddenly as they had started.

The Escalade was where it had been before the fireworks started—halfway up the hill.

The four of them stayed in the vehicle. There was that putrid smell that comes after fireworks display. Given the smoke, the smell, and the setting, everything appeared surreal.

It was then I notice them.

Stationed all around the ridge at the top of the bowl were men dressed in green Army fatigues, green T-shirts and green baseball caps, with green bandanas covering their faces. I counted eight of them, spaced evenly. I looked closer and four of them had sawed-off shotguns, one had a long-barrel rifle and the other three had handguns.

The two with the shotguns and the two with the handguns came down from their spots with their guns raised. There was a military manner about them. They surrounded the Escalade.

The remaining shotgun and the two handguns came down to surround Squal and me. In both cases they came down from the hill in such a way as to cover all directions.

Curtis emerged from the Escalade holding a handgun.

"Get the fuck out with your hands high!" the first guy with the handgun said. The four of them kept their firearms pointed at the Escalade. They held the firearms in both hands, like they had had training. Curtis dropped the gun.

The remaining three stood in front of Squal and me. They didn't say anything. I got the impression they were waiting for orders.

The guy who had ordered them out of the Escalade spoke. "Allow me to introduce myself. I am Raheen and I lead the Green Street Gangstars. I am here to let you know that you are doing business on our land and that is not allowed." He walked to the Escalade and as he did, the other gunmen took a step closer to the car.

Raheen pulled out the duffel bag.

"We will be taking this because it is ours." He put the shoulder strap across his back and carried the satchel. "Cover them," he commanded the others.

He came down the hill to where we were standing.

His men parted so he could get a closer look at us. As he approached, something began to go off in my head just a little. He looked vaguely familiar. When I say vaguely, I mean vaguely because my thought processes weren't functioning at their peak.

"And you two with the product. You are opening up business in Green Street territory. That can't be allowed. That simply—" He stopped abruptly and stared right at me. He tilted his head like something didn't seem to fit just right. "Duffy?"

I didn't get a chance to answer or confirm his inquiry.

"Right there! Drop it!" I turned and it was Kurth. He was alone but he had a gun trained on Raheen.

A cascade of gunfire from Raheen's men, those close by and those next to the car, rained down. Kurth's body was torn to shreds as it buckled and seized under the gunfire. It was a horrible sight.

That acrid smell that comes from fireworks and guns filled the air, making me want to throw up. There was a wispy cloud of smoke that filled the small circle around Kurth's body, Squal, the Green Streeters and me.

The surreal and violent scene, along with the out-and-out assault on the senses, would make the hardest soldier, cop or wise guy lose his concentration. It gave Renzo the chance he needed.

I saw him take off down the hill, and by the time they opened fire, he had become too hard to hit. He was back in the brush and he had a thirty-foot head start.

I took off after him.

Chapter Thirty-Five

"Stay!" Raheen commanded. "Hold your fire!" I heard as I tore after Renzo.

He was smart enough not to run along the trails. That would be easy, but it also would be easy to track. I could hear his movement through the brush as sticks and branches broke under his feet. I followed the sounds the best I could, but it was difficult to work up any speed while hurdling downed trees and swatting branches from my head.

I kept moving, scratches accumulating across my head and arms, until I could no longer hear him. Now I was just running straight ahead, without knowing whether I was even going in the right direction. My chest heaved and I was covered in sweat. After another twenty feet I got the sinking feeling that I had lost him. I stopped and stood in the center of the woods, unable to see five feet in front of me. I was exhausted and lost, and more important, I had lost Renzo. I felt a mix of desperation and terror.

It didn't last for long.

Without warning I felt a force crash down on me from above. He came out of the oak tree above me, landed on my shoulders and wrestled me to the ground. He rolled over on top of me, used his left hand to steady himself, and punched me hard in the jaw with his right.

That too-familiar flash of light ran through my brain and made me instantly nauseous. Even in my stupor I recognized another one of these and knew it would be lights out, maybe forever. Renzo pulled back his right fist, and as he did, I swung my left arm around his left, locked his elbow and gave it everything I had to stand with his elbow locked.

He yelled in pain and I was able to turn him over. Now I was on top and I hit him with a four-punch, piston-like combination to the center of his face. I felt and heard his nose crackle and blood exploded over both of us. I paused for just a second to throw another combo and he was somehow able to grab my throat. It was enough for me to lose my balance and fall off him. I rolled over and got to my feet. Renzo could fight and knew how to fight dirty.

Now we were circling each other.

"You couldn't leave well enough alone, could you?" He had his guard up and moved on his feet like he'd had training. I didn't answer him.

I did a quick shuffle step in and threw a triple jab with my right. He was ready for the first and parried it; the second one glanced off his guard and landed on his cheek with a quarter of the force. He hadn't expected the third, which landed on his already-broken nose. Instinctively, he brought his hands to his face.

Just what I wanted.

I dropped a straight left into his solar plexus, and he coughed a sick cough and I thought he would puke. With his hands to his stomach, I whipped a left around to his liver. It did what it was supposed to do, and I said a silent prayer to the Mexican guys in Vegas who had taught it to me.

He collapsed, defeated.

I put my right knee on his chest and my left hand on his throat. I put enough pressure on the throat to make his eyes bulge as he felt the pain and the fear.

It didn't last long.

I heard the clackety-clack of a firearm and when I looked up, Curtis was pointing his sawed-off shotgun at me from twenty feet.

"Get the fuck off him!" He yelled.

I paused for a second to think. He fired one past my ear.

I got off of Renzo, who spat and coughed and rolled over. He coughed for about five straight minutes until he rolled over, gathered himself and got to his feet.

It was Curtis and Renzo, a shotgun and me.

I didn't like my odds.

Chapter Thirty-Six

"Time to say goodbye, Asshole," Curtis said. He took a step forward and brought the gun up to aim.

"Hold it!" Renzo yelled through a scraggly voice. "Not just yet." His nose was a bloody mess, broken and spread all over his face.

He came over and punched me hard in the face. I had my hands up and a shotgun aimed at my head. I went down. I threw up and the whole world started to spin.

"Piece of shit," Renzo said. "You couldn't leave it alone."

"Fuck you," I said. If I was going to die, I was going to die fighting. He kicked me in the stomach.

"AJ, fuckin AJ, all of this for fucking AJ," he said. He had gathered himself, and his arrogance was back. "AJ knew to play the game. He did okay. But you—you stupid piece of shit."

I looked at him.

"What game did you have AJ playing?" I asked. I wanted to bide what time I had left.

He laughed. "Yeah, doesn't make any difference now, does it? Nah, it really doesn't." He kicked at the ground a little bit and took an overdramatic look at the sky. "I was there with Barnes, the pharmacist at the store. We were going over our plans, and we look up, and there's the dumb fuck candy man. He'd heard everything. He knew what we were doing. That couldn't be allowed."

"Why didn't you kill him?" I asked.

"Too risky. Too many people saw him on his route. Now his family...that's another story," He laughed. "You make it clear you're going to get after a man's wife and three-year-old—you pretty much can do whatever you want."

"So he had to move away. Leave his family behind. And you made sure you kept him reminded with your visits and Christmas cards." It was all coming into focus.

"It isn't complicated." Renzo said it with such bravado it made me sick.

"And Barnes?"

"Oh, Barnes came willingly. The guy's a genius. We got him to create the analogs...M-Sixteen...Uzi, the possibilities are endless. He gets paid real well, his kid is taken care of for life, and he takes on a new identity—that is, until you fucked this all up. Then you want to get the business. You're a fucking fool, Duffy."

"And the pain clinics?" I had to know.

"Shit, they're easy. Those fuckers are so in debt and so eager to make money. You turn them on to how easy life can be and then you have them. They're in deep and there's nothing they can do. They're licensed, they make money and we make money."

"Nice and tidy for you. And what about the O-Ds, the ruined lives?"

"C'mon, Asshole. They're all going to get high anyway. We don't have to go looking. They come to us."

He paused and looked at Curtis. "I'm getting bored talking to him. Let's do it and get the fuck out of these woods."

Curtis smiled out of one corner of his mouth. He made a big deal out of slowly raising the gun, trying to be nonchalant.

I had one chance and it wasn't a good one.

I ran at him with everything I had, screaming and waving my arms.

I heard the deafening bang and then a second one as I leaped at Curtis.

I missed and I crashed to the ground.

I didn’t feel anything.
Then I looked up.

Chapter Thirty-Seven

It was Kyrone.

His handgun was down by his side and he stared straight ahead. He had no expression on his face. Squal came running up behind him.

"Duff, Jesus, you all right?" Squal said.

"Holy shit for two thousand, Alex," I said. "You got that right."

Kyrone stared straight ahead.

"He deserved to die—motherfucker deserved to die..." Kyrone was almost catatonic. I don't think he was aware of anyone else but himself, and Renzo and Curtis's remains.

"Your buddy here is a bit of an eavesdropper. He caught all of our plans last night at the bar. Took it upon himself to show up," Squal said.

"...and bring a gun." It was a point I thought needed to be added.

"Yeah, there's that," Squal said.

We stood there in silence for a long moment. Kyrone broke out of his catatonia. He held the gun away from himself and looked at it like it wasn't his hand holding it. He slowly changed his focus and looked at me.

"Kyrone, you saved my life," I said.

"I owed you that. You saved mine. For a while, you had Latanya saved but..." he didn't finish. He dropped to his knees and began to cry. We let him.

"Hey, Duff," Squal said. "I don't want to burden you with details, especially now, but one of those gangbangers recognized you. You know him?"

"He looked familiar, but I couldn't place him."

Right on cue we heard the sound of company joining us in the woods. I was too much in shock and too tired to move. It was three Green Streeters.

Instinctively, I put my hands in the air. Squal and Kyrone followed suit. The lead guy looked at Renzo.

"He dead?"

"Yes," I said.

"Saved us some work. So are the rest of them." He took some time to take it all in.

"Thanks, Duff. We got to get out of here but there was somethin' unfinished." He pulled his bandana down. He looked really familiar.

"Uh, don't thank me. Kyrone's the one who saved the day." I nodded toward Kyrone.

"Yeah?" He looked over to Kyrone. "My Man, thank you. You ever need Green Street, you shout, got it?"

Kyrone nodded and half-smiled.

"Duff, you don't remember, huh?" he laughed. "Shony's cousin? Raheen."

It came back to me. "Of course, Man. Now I remember."

"Yo, the bag!" He yelled.

One of the Green Streeters handed him the duffel.

"We gonna keep the product. Normally, we'd keep this, too, but we's honorable," He gave me a big toothy smile flashing his gold tooth. He threw me the duffel with the quarter million in it.

I just looked at him.

"I remember Shony. I remember you the only one who cared to go get her. I remember," he said.

"That was fifteen years ago..."

"I remember..."

Sirens could be heard in the distance.

"That's our signal. Peace out..." The three of them took off in different directions and it was only seconds before they were invisible. They were like—no, they were trained soldiers.

"You got some interesting contacts, Duff," Squal said.

"*What is dumb luck for two thousand*," I said.

"A true Daily Double."

"You guys get out. I'll stick around to talk to law enforcement. Kelley should be here any second.

"C'mon Kyrone," Squal said, and they started their trot out of the woods.

I headed back to the reservoir.

Chapter Thirty-Eight

By now the bowl was swarming with cops. I walked out of the clearing with my hands up, just to be on the safe side.

"On the ground! Face on the ground! Now!" came the command from an exuberant guy in tactical gear. There were four of them with their guns trained on me. I was starting to get used to it.

"Hold your fire! Hold your fire!" came the call from a familiar voice. I was able to peek up and see Detective Mike Kelley approaching the four men. He talked to the guy who had yelled the command.

"Stand down! Stand down!" came the following call.

I will undoubtedly take shit from him later but when the shit hit the fan, it was good to have Kelley around. He approached me, along with a guy wearing an FBI windbreaker.

"Are you armed?" The FBI guy said.

"No, Sir," I said.

"Get up slowly. Let us see your hands the whole way." He spoke clearly and with confidence. This was obviously what he did.

"I'm sorry about Agent Kurth," I said, remembering him getting blown away.

"Shut up!" the agent said with a distinct change in control.

"What?" I said reflexively.

"Not now, Duff," Kelley said firmly. Experience had told me

to do what Kelley said in such circumstances.

"Renzo is dead. So is his guy, Curtis. They're back in the woods," I said. I guessed that was worth violating the silence order.

The agent asked where and he and his men went to see.

"Stay with him," The agent commanded Kelley.

It was just me and Kelley.

"Why did the guy freak when I mentioned Kurth?"

Kelley just looked at me. He didn't say anything for a long time. Finally, he spoke.

"Kurth wasn't D-E-A," he said.

"Huh?"

"He was a fake. He was with the Chicago outfit. It was a set-up." Kelley exhaled.

"What? But why?" It didn't make any sense.

"He had fake credentials. There were fake phone calls from his superiors to the chief. We think they wanted to make an easy score on someone who wasn't in the typical drug business. They found you."

"What the..."

"You gave them a quarter of a million dollars for baby laxative. They were ripping you off—not getting you and your buddy Squal into the drug business. It was a high-level con."

I didn't know what to say or how to feel.

"It turned into a shit show when the Green Street Gangstars showed up. They decided to go to war to protect their turf. You have any idea how they would've got tipped off about the deal?"

I just looked at him. I had no idea.

"You've been visiting your Albino friend, haven't you? You think the Caretaker knew anything about this?"

"I got the money from him." I didn't lie to Kelley. I figured giving me money wasn't a crime. Kelley rolled his eyes.

"His niece was one of the recent O-Ds, right?"

"Yeah."

"And she was gonna marry that guy that comes in and drinks the coffee with all the sugars, right?"

"Yeah.

"Uh-huh. It is right about here that you would probably prefer that I stop asking you questions, right?" Kelley looked straight at me.

"I've never lied to you, Kel." It was the truth.

"Let's not get into the semantics of lying by omission."

"Probably not a good idea," I said.

"Uh-huh."

My mind went back to my meeting with the pain doctor and his description. It fit.

"Shit, Kelley, he fits the description the guy at the pain clinic gave me. I never gave it a thought."

"Well, that would tie it together, wouldn't it? Fair bet it's him." Kelley shook his head and winced. "Pretty embarrassing for the force."

"I bet." I didn't know what to say and I wanted to avoid anything that could be interpreted as piling on.

Kelley changed the subject.

"Look, I can run interference for you as much as I can, but you're going to have to answer a shitload of questions from a shit load of different types of cops."

"Yeah, I've been through it before."

"Uh-huh. I'm gonna skip the lectures, Duff, but really? Can this be the end of your Robin-Hood-Hero bullshit?" Kelley looked right at me.

I shrugged. I didn't lie to him.

"Yeah, that's what I thought. No real point in asking, is there?" Kelley said. He didn't exactly smile. It was more of a smirk. "You got anything else you want to tell me?"

He could sense I was leaving something out.

I just shook my head.

I thought about Kyrone. He had saved my life. He or The Caretaker or both probably had something to do with orchestrating the Green Street Gangstars. I probably would never get the full story. I was okay with that. Mostly. I liked to know how everything fit together but I didn't need to know, especially if the people that I wanted to be safe were made safe.

Would Kyrone be smart enough to get rid of the gun? Would he avoid being picked up and tested for firing it? He had to know it would be traced. Kyrone might not know how to stay clean and sober but he knew the street and how to survive on it. I guessed he'd be all right.

I would love to know how he knew to show up.

Chapter Thirty-Nine

Kelley was right. I spent the entire overnight answering questions. It was exhausting and tedious, answering the same questions over and over. I tried to remember that people were dead, and this was the price I paid for, as Kelley might say, my Robin-Hood-Hero bullshit.

My story was the shots that killed Renzo most likely came from one of the Green Street Gangstars. I kept saying that their bandanas covered their faces, and I could only describe their outfits. They asked me about their voices, their height and build and I gave them some answers. They knew the Green Streeters, and they knew the gang knew what they were doing, so even though they pressed me for answers, I could sense they knew they weren't going to get anything they didn't already know.

As for my goal of being truthful, well, I'm not above rationalization. Maybe Kyrone had some connection to the gang. It was plausible, though unlikely, but it wasn't an out-and-out lie.

If I were a smarter dude, I'd talk to myself about moral relativism.

Sometimes there were advantages to not being so smart.

When I finally got back home, the dogs were pacing back and forth. They were hungry, had full bladders and were out of sync with their schedule, which did not make for calm and obedient companions. I leashed them up and got them out of the apartment as fast as I could. They both pee'd and pooped almost immediately. I let them stretch their legs a bit more and then it was back to the apartment for an extra-large meal to make up for the one they'd skipped. Extra-large meals helped ease the guilt I felt for leaving them alone.

I was banged up and sore from my fight with Renzo. I've had it worse, but it was going to take more than a few days to get over all of this. It always did. I knew what to expect from the physical healing process. It was the mental and emotional scarring that left me a little more bewildered. I could never tell what it would take to heal that way.

I sat with a cup of coffee and went over my to-do list. Nearly getting killed kind of puts things in perspective, and some decisions become much easier to take. I needed to talk to AJ's daughter and, whether she wanted to hear it or not, straighten out what she thought she knew about her father.

I had to get down to the gym and let them know I wasn't the guy to replace Smitty.

And I had to sell the bar.

Chapter Forty

I got to the Y about three o'clock and decided to get a workout in before I met with the director to decline the job. It may have been a bit of procrastination, but it was also about loosening up my sore body to speed the recovery along. I think the fancy term is "active rest," meaning you go through the motions enough to break a sweat and warm up the muscles with similar activity that made you sore in the first place. I was going to leave out the being shot at part in my active-rest session.

Workouts like this started slowly and awkwardly, but in ten or fifteen minutes I'd warm and the whole activity would start to feel worthwhile. At the beginning it seemed like a stupid idea, but I had enough experience to give it some time before quitting. In the end it was worth dealing with some temporary discomfort.

The idea of a nice little shake out warm-up went out the window when I entered the gym. The music, if you could call it that, blared, and Lorenzo and his sycophants danced like they owned the place. They were loud and stupid, and they acted like no one else belonged there.

I put my gear down and tried to ignore them, but it was next to impossible. They mocked other guys who were just working out with inside jokes to one another, and I saw a couple of guys leave earlier than they would have normally. I swore a couple of them gave me a look on the way out. It was a look of desperation and a little disappointment that I had let them down.

Again, it made me a little sick to my stomach. I told myself this wasn't my battle. This wasn't my gym, and it wasn't my duty to do anything but get a workout. I wrapped my hands, put on my headphones and started to shake out and get loose. I did my best to ignore Lorenzo's group, and the headphones helped a little, but if I played a quieter song their shit intruded. I watched Lorenzo from the corner of my eye as he worked the heavy bag. He was not only gifted athletically, he could hit hard, which is a different skill set all together. The room actually shook as he worked on the bag.

I saw Billy come through the door, and he walked over and we bumped fists. He glanced at Lorenzo and the boys, looked at me and frowned. I shrugged my shoulders. Billy had been at the gym a decade less than I had, but he valued what Smitty had set up. The fact that I was letting Billy down in some way or that something that had changed Billy's life so much was going away ate at me. It ate at me really bad.

The round sounded and I moved over to the rope. I switched up my playlist to fast Elvis songs. "Burnin' Love," "Suspicious Minds," "Promised Land" and "Washed My Hands In Dirty Water" played and set the tempo like they always did. I was having trouble getting a groove and kept missing skips. That was usually a sign that my concentration and flow were off. It wasn't hard to understand why.

The choir was singing the bridge in "Burnin' Love" when I watched Lorenzo go over to Wally, a relatively new guy at the gym. Wally had been boxing for six months, was fat and not very good. He was kind of slow mentally and tended to talk about winning the heavyweight championship in a few years. No one took him seriously or ever took offense to it because they knew Wally didn't really know any better.

I took my headphones off because I wanted to hear the interactions.

"Hey, Wal-man, how about we do some light stuff, you know,

to keep sharp. Nothin' heavy," Lorenzo said. It wasn't uncommon for guys of different abilities to get in the ring together. Still, I didn't trust this. I didn't trust this at all.

Billy looked at Lorenzo for a long moment and then looked at me. I didn't know what to say.

Lorenzo and Wally gloved up and climbed through the ropes. Wally looked excited and flattered to be in the ring with an up-and-coming star, and I imagined he was honored to be asked to share the ring with Lorenzo. Smitty had always been very careful about who he'd allow Wally to work with. He certainly wouldn't have allowed this.

It started off slowly like it should have and I felt myself relax just a little. Lorenzo had spent enough time in gyms, and he knew how things went. His boys had gathered around the ring like they always did to cheer him on. Wally was clumsy and moved the best he could, but he didn't know what he was doing so most things were wrong. Every time he'd throw a punch, Lorenzo would already have moved to another spot. He was incredibly quick and after a few times, there was an exaggeration to how much Wally missed him by. The boys laughed.

That seemed to fuel Lorenzo.

Now Lorenzo was stepping it up a bit. He slipped a slow hook from Wally, pivoted, planted and threw a right hand. It was a full-power swing, and Wally went down. Lorenzo did an exaggerated Ali-shuffle while Wally struggled to get up.

"C'mom Fat Boy, you gots to learn to take a punch." Lorenzo's crew laughed and high-fived.

I was getting sick to my stomach.

Lorenzo was now working the jab, and each time he did he yelled, "Pop!" and then laughed. On every third one, he'd throw a right hand and catch Wally flush with full power. The third time he did it Wally went down again, and Lorenzo mocked him like he was Liston after Ali had dropped him. Then he laughed.

Billy looked at me. He looked at me real hard.

Wally was struggling to get up. There were two minutes left

in the round. That's a lot of time to take a beating.

Billy looked at me, hesitated and then spoke. "You know, Duff, you saved my life and I love you for it." He paused. He might have had a hard time speaking. "Sometimes we don't choose when we have to be a leader." He just looked at me after that. After a long moment he looked back at the ring. Wally was getting up.

I went over and turned off the electronic timer.

The gym got quiet, real quiet, and everyone stopped working. Even Lorenzo's crew went silent. I could feel the eyes on me.

"Yo, Duffy, what the fuck are you doin'? It's the middle of the round!" Lorenzo said with a laugh. "I need my work," he laughed again, and the guys laughed with him.

"Wally, take a break. I need a little work," I said.

Wally stepped between the ropes, catching his foot coming out. He stumbled a little and some of Lorenzo's buddies tittered at that. Guys who never got in the ring.

"Don't take off your gear yet," I called to Wally. He shrugged and sniffed a bit. I hoped it was from exertion and not from tears. "Billy, get me Smitty's gear."

Billy looked surprised but he went ahead. He gloved me up with Smitty's old gear and went to put on the headgear. Quietly and well under the music, I said, "Don't do the buckle all the way on the chin strap."

Billy got a strange look on his face but did as I asked.

"Me and you, Duff?" Lorenzo said with a bit of a smile. "Let's do it!"

I felt everyone in the gym slowly crowd around like they naturally do when something is happening in the ring. It was a feeling more than a perception.

I didn't say anything. Lorenzo was twenty-five years younger than I, but a grown man. He was on the way up and my prime, whenever that was, had been a while back. I ignored him and turned to Wally.

"Hit the bell, Wally," I said.

I moved toward Lorenzo slowly and methodically with my

hands down around my waist. He threw a hard jab that landed flush on my cheek and I heard the onlookers react. I continued forward and he threw two more, both landing. I kept moving toward him.

"Throw the right," I said quietly. Lorenzo had had seventeen knockouts in his amateur career, all with his right hand. He threw it and it landed just above my right ear. It hurt and it made my head swim, but after years of doing this, I knew how to conceal it. I didn't raise my guard and I didn't step back. I knew what that would do.

Lorenzo started to twitch a little. It happens in a way that only years in the ring will show you. I know what I did. I just let him hit with his five best shots and, as far as he could tell, it did nothing to me.

I tapped the ball of my left foot on the canvass. It helped me remember the ideal stance. I moved my hips so that my body swayed a little from left to right and I felt the momentum build. Lorenzo wasn't throwing. He became a bit tentative. I waited. My head swam from the shots I'd let him land and I knew I couldn't take many more of those. It was time.

I moved closer, almost like I was setting him up for a body shot. I had my guard in a Ken Norton-style peek-a-boo, and I knew I had to do it quickly. I pushed up my right, moving the top of the headgear off of my forehead, took a lunge in and brought the crown of my head down on Lorenzo's nose with everything I had.

I heard the snap, then I heard him wail in pain.

He went down on one knee.

The gym went silent.

"Get up." I commanded.

Lorenzo got to his feet. His nose was bent and was now almost parallel with his face. Blood completely covered his nose and chin, and his shirt was stained.

He put his guard over his face, which I knew he would. There was still a minute and half to go in the round.

I threw to his body as fast and as hard as I could until he collapsed. He threw up on the canvas. He was gagging on his own vomit.

"Stop the round" I called out. Billy hit the timer.

"Get up," I said. "Get up!" I knew it was a request he couldn't fulfill for another minute or two, but I repeated it. I wanted the gym to not only see what was happening but to hear it.

"Get up!" This time I awkwardly pulled him up, grabbing him under his arms and leaning him against the ropes. He was doubled over.

I threw another hook to his side. He collapsed again and cried out loud.

I stood over him for a full minute.

"Get up," I said, this time more quietly. He crawled a few steps and then got to his feet.

"Wally!" I yelled. "Finish my round."

Wally looked startled. He climbed through the ropes with some apprehension.

As I passed him on my way out of the ring, I touched him on the shoulder and gave him some direction.

"I'd go to his body," I said.

Lorenzo was barely standing. He was still mostly doubled over but he couldn't raise his arms.

Wally drove a right into his body. Lorenzo blocked most of it, but the force pushed his arm into his side. Wally windmilled a left-right-left-left-right, back and forth on Lorenzo's sides. It was awkward as hell and as fundamentally incorrect as punches could be.

It didn't matter.

Lorenzo gasped and collapsed again.

The bell rang to end the round.

"That's enough for today, Wally," I said on my way into the ring.

I knelt over Lorenzo. He was trying to catch his breath.

"Get the fuck out of my gym," I said. It was loud enough for everyone to hear. "You hear me? Get the fuck out of my gym!"

I stepped out of the ring.

I walked past Lorenzo's crew, who didn't know where to look. I got to the speaker that was playing the music. I picked it up with both hands, held it way over my head, and slammed it into the floor. I did it three times until the music completely stopped.

"If you're gonna work out in my gym, you're going to have to follow the rules." I scanned everyone in the gym and made sure I made eye contact with all of them. Then I headed into Smitty's office.

Chapter Forty-One

My heart continued to pound for a long time after that, and I decided to put off my official meeting with the director. It wasn't the time to have any formal discussions.

Instead, I headed to Galway Lake. The ride and Elvis would help me chill out and give me some time to think. On the way, I got to thinking about AJ and what he had asked me to do. He hadn't been very specific but somehow, he knew that I'd fix things for him. Things he couldn't have fixed while he was on this plane, but things that maybe I could. I wanted the man to rest, knowing he'd done the best he could.

He'd done what he'd done to keep his family safe. It had been a sad and impossible decision, and it made me understand why he had been in a perpetually bad mood. What he'd done, estranging himself from his wife and daughter to protect them, was nothing less than an expression of love.

That line of thinking brought me to Barnes. Did he do what he'd done out of love? He'd wanted to provide for his son, and maybe he knew he wasn't emotionally capable of doing any more than that, so he did what lots of dads did—he made as much money as he could, worked his ass off, and provided. Maybe he knew this would be the best life for the kid. Rather than step up and try to be a dad to a kid with lots of needs, had delegated it. Not hard to see how he could arrive at that rationalization. Maybe losing his wife had just been too much for him.

How he could rationalize making a drug that caused so much pain was a little harder to process. Maybe it was about his knowing that addicts were going to use anyway. He wouldn't have to see it firsthand, he'd just play in his laboratory. It was kind of like the military guys who steer drones from thousands of miles away and set them up to blow away entire cities. They didn't get their hands dirty and it didn't make them late for lunch.

People's capacity for rationalization was endless.

He'd have a long time to think about that.

The pain doctor was off the hook. It would be up to him to right his ship, now that he had the bad guys off his back. He was going to lose out on the revenue, and he'd have to deal with that. We'd have to wait and see.

I guess it was a matter of faith.

My faith in the goodness of people wasn't real strong.

And what to make of my friend The Caretaker? I got to see a little behind the curtain at the unmasked character. No defenses, just some raw emotion that I didn't think he really had. In the end, he was just as much feeling flesh and blood as the rest of us. Maybe his defenses kept some deep emotion at bay all the time. When I thought of it, no one would curate such an elaborate persona without the need to. Made me wonder what The Caretaker's life had been about when he'd just been Dush.

Then there was Kyrone. The man had his demons but there was no denying his strengths and his commitment to love and the people who were dear to him. Where the drugs fit in was hard to figure, except for the guess that he had a lot of feeling going on, too. I guess we all did. Whether killing Renzo would exorcise his demons remained to be seen. Life keeps moving on and it has a way of conjuring up new demons, or at least the old demons in new disguises. I wished sobriety and peace for Kyrone, but I wasn't confident he'd get it any more than anyone else would.

It was a grey overcast day, even though the radio told me it was going to be partly sunny. The lake reflected the grey and seemed not to have the color of just a week ago. It amazed me how seasons seemed to change in an instant, even though I knew they inched along. Maybe it was our perception that woke up to what was changing around us.

I spotted Amy at the side of her house. She was raking again, perpetually gathering leaves, trying to stay ahead of the season. The beauty of the trees demanded their due at the end of every fall. There was a price to be paid for everything.

"What do you want?" she asked. I watched her sigh and shake her head.

"You need to listen. This won't take long, but you need to listen," I said.

She rolled her eyes.

I talked for about ten minutes straight while she remained silent.

"Your dad went away because he stumbled across something bad through no fault of his own. Some bad people threatened to harm you and your mom, and they made sure he left town and didn't come back. They were mob guys from Chicago. Bad men, killers, and they let your dad know that they would hurt you if he stayed around. It was about the drug trade and exploiting the most vulnerable of people. They visited him every month and sent him Christmas cards and pictures to let him know they were watching. He had to leave to protect yout. So, he left. He asked me through a note to find out and somehow fix it. With a lot of help, I did. He did the best he could in a horrible situation. He did what he did out of love. He did it because of his love for you and your mother."

I stopped talking. She looked at me. Then she turned and looked out at the lake. The sky was still a slate grey, but there seemed to be some brightness behind the clouds. She turned back and looked down briefly and then up at me. There were tears in her eyes. She didn't acknowledge them.

She exhaled hard and adjusted her grip on the rake.

"Thank you," she said. She went back to raking.

I walked back to the Cadillac.

Chapter Forty-Two

On the way back I decided it was as good a time as any to tell the guys I couldn't keep the bar. I didn't have any idea what was for me now, but it wasn't the bar.

This just wasn't for me.

They'd be upset but they'd understand. I'd keep it open until I found a buyer and they'd still have a place to come. I knew it wouldn't cease being AJ's, but in a sense, it already had. They'd understand. They'd go to another place and make it their own.

Billy had covered the place for me today while I took my road trip. It was after seven when I got back, but he didn't care. He smiled when I came around the bar and we bumped fists.

"Uh, you're going to have to show me some of the technique you used today in the ring," he said, and smiled.

"Son, there are some things that shouldn't be taught," I said.

"Somebody taught you."

I thought about that for a minute.

"Yeah, he did."

Billy laughed and slapped me on the back.

"Someday?" Billy said.

"Someday," I said.

There was a moment of silence between the two of us and it allowed for Rocco's narrative to come through.

"So anyway, the munchkins were giving all of Oz the finger," Rocco said. It wasn't the first time *The Wizard of Oz* had been the focus of discussion. I doubted it would be the last.

"We've been over this. They were having problems with the small people's union," Jerry Number One said.

"Little," Jerry Number Two said.

"Well, it may seem little to you, but it was a real labor issue!" Rocco said.

"They're not called 'small' people. It's 'little' people," Jerry Number Two said.

The other three just stared at him.

"Anyway, they were trying to decide if they should join the Lollipop Guild or the Teamsters," Rocco said.

"The Lollipop Guild was just in the movie," TC said.

"Exactly," Rocco said with satisfaction. "That was why there was unrest."

And so it went.

I was getting ready to tell them. Rocco interrupted before I could.

"Hey, he's here!" he yelled.

"He's been here for twenty minutes—you never stopped talking," TC said.

"Billy, go get it!" Rocco said and rubbed his hands together.

I had no idea what was going on. Billy came back with a huge flat thing, awkwardly wrapped.

"For you, Duff, from all of us," Rocco said.

I tore the paper off of it. It was a hand-carved wooden sign in green and gold, shaped like a pair of boxing gloves. It said: "Duffy's Bar." In smaller letters at the bottom, it said: "At AJ's."

"For the front of the place," TC said.

I didn't know what to say. Holy shit, I didn't know what to say!

"Fellas, I'm speechless," I said. Something caught in my throat and I couldn't speak for a full moment. "I really, really appreciate it."

It was all I could say.

I set everyone up with a drink and cracked open a Schlitz for myself. The guys were all smiling.

I was finishing my beer when Squal came in. I cracked a Narragansett. "You gotta put it on! It's about to start! It's my night!" he said, with more than a little desperation.

"Huh? Oh, shit! It's your *Jeopardy!* night!" I switched the channel.

Sure enough, there he was with Ken Jennings. He had the middle spot, and he was wearing a suit with a black shirt and a black tie. It was surreal and hard to believe.

He crushed "Potent Potables," "Football Follies" and "U.S. Government." He struggled with a category on sitcoms and another on soccer. He was doing great, concentrating really hard and giving it everything he had.

Still, he was behind and in third place going into Final Jeopardy.

The Final Jeopardy question—er, answer—was: "From Twelfth Night, Malvolia offers this quote in mockery of a dire situation..."

The bar was silent.

Squal didn't give it away.

Jennings called on the other contestants, who were both ahead of Squal.

The current champion answered, "Dost thou think, because thou art virtuous, there shall be no more cakes and ale?"

Jennings told him he was wrong. But he had wagered only a dollar.

Squal was in trouble.

The second contestant answered, "Better a witty fool than a foolish wit."

Jennings consoled him, but he, too, had wagered only a dollar.

Then, Jennings went to Squal, who answered: "What is, 'Some men are born great while others have greatness thrust upon them.'"

"That's right!" Jennings exclaimed. "Let's see how much you wagered."

Squal had bet all of it. He'd gone all in.

Of course, he had. He had come out the winner.

He wasn't the only one.

TOM SCHRECK is the author of Amazon's #1 hard-boiled mystery, *The Vegas Knockout*. He counts Robert B. Parker, John D. MacDonald, JA Konrath, Reed Farrel Coleman, Ken Bruen and Michael Connelly among his favorite crime fiction authors and his Duffy Dombrowski series has been referred to as "As good or better as the early Spenser." He is a columnist with Westchester Magazine and a frequent contributor to Crimespree Magazine, Referee, and other publications.

On the following pages are a few more great titles from the Down & Out Books publishing family.

For a complete list of books and to sign up for our newsletter, go to DownAndOutBooks.com.

A Semblance of Control
Mark T. Conard

Down & Out Books
June 2023
978-1-64396-302-0

One night Jake Micallef does a little breaking-and-entering and stumbles upon a plot to assassinate his estranged brother, who just happens to be the Mayor of New York City.

As Jake wrestles with that bombshell, another one walks straight into his life: Marcie Yates. Marcie eerily resembles Jake's old girlfriend, the woman who helped his brother tear his world apart. But when thugs kidnap Marcie to keep Jake from interfering in the assassination plot, he has no choice but to track down the conspirators, only to discover he's fallen right into their trap. In the end, Jake must risk everything to save Marcie and stop the bullet headed for his brother.

Crime Under the Sun
A Sisters in Crime Anthology
Edited by Matt Coyle, Naomi Hirahara
and Tammy Kaehler

Down & Out Books
July 2023
978-1-64396-322-8

In *Crime Under the Sun*, the second anthology offered by Partners in Crime, the San Diego chapter of Sisters in Crime, fifteen stories capture the hopes and dreams of characters trying to live the idyllic SoCal life. Instead, they bump up against greed, treachery, corruption, and murder.

These stories will thrill readers with unexpected twists and turns and surprise endings.

Psycho Therapy
A Diamond Mystery
TG Wolff

Down & Out Books
July 2023
978-1-64396-323-5

An intervention puts Diamond on a therapist's couch, dropping her in a high-stakes game of blackmail, kidnapping, and murder.

From a video gaming Beastmaster in Michigan, to a suicide bomber in Virginia, to a psychiatric conference in France, Diamond jumps in with her usual flair for chaos and destruction.

Just as she is about to win, Fate rears up, inserting a knife and twisting.

The Spread
A Penns River Crime Novel
Dana King

Down & Out Books
July 2023
978-1-64396-324-2

A gambling ring based on local high school football leads to murder and turmoil in Penns River while a routine civilian ride-along results in controversy and a formal complaint.

Crime continues to evolve in Penns River, stressing the police department more all the time as retirements create a departmental transition the town is ill-equipped to handle gracefully.

"Dana King writes in a gritty crime noir style with a modern flair all his own. His books grab you from the first page and don't let you go." —Terrence McCauley, award-winning author of thrillers, crime and westerns

Printed in the USA
CPSIA information can be obtained
at www.ICGtesting.com
LVHW080239031123
762890LV00003B/368